Pseudonym Maskman

The dead shot: Sportsman's complete guide

Being a treatise on the use of the gun

Pseudonym Maskman

The dead shot: Sportsman's complete guide
Being a treatise on the use of the gun

ISBN/EAN: 9783337198206

Printed in Europe, USA, Canada, Australia, Japan

Cover: Foto ©Andreas Hilbeck / pixelio.de

More available books at **www.hansebooks.com**

ADVERTISEMENT.

THE enthusiastic greeting with which this admirable treatise has been welcomed by the British sportsmen, and the united commendations it has elicited from the English press, has induced the Publisher to offer it to American sportsmen, feeling assured it will be as gratefully accepted by them.

This reprint is from the latest carefully revised edition, the illustrated attitudes and positions have been carefully redrawn and engraved by our best artists; and no pains have been spared in reproducing it in a style worthy its mérits and character.

Although FRANK FORESTER's "Complete Manual for Young Sportsmen" is the acknowledged authority in this country on this and kindred topics, much new information will be found embodied in the "Dead Shot," discovered since the former work was prepared, relating to improvements in breech-loading arms and other useful information of advantage to the new beginner, and worth the attention of the mature sportsman. One of the most valuable features of the book is

that which treats of the flight of gan
that has not been so fully discussed
works on the science of shooting.

There is nothing comparable to
common sense rules contained in his
lessons on the art of shooting; and
regards his thoroughly practical finis
preparing his pupil by degrees, when
his precepts, to become proficient as

The Author "has purposely excl
ject of wild-fowl shooting" becaus
works fully describe this particula
wild-fowler, and all who are inter
branch of shooting, will find it elabo
in FRANK FORESTER's "Field Sport

For the better comprehension of
little manual, and for the purpose
of practical utility to the American sp
following extract from FRANK FOR
duction to "The Dog," by Dinks,
Hutchinson, is appended; explanato
ferences and comparative relations o
American game.

"I will conclude by observing, th
this work is exclusively on breaking
shooting, there is not one word in it
applicable to this country.

"The methods of woodcock and snipe shooting are **exactly** the same in both countries, excepting only that in England there is no **summer-cock** shooting. Otherwise, the practice, the **rules,** and qualifications of dogs are identical.

" The partridge in England, varies in **few of** its **habits** from our quail; I might almost say in none, unless that it prefers turnip **fields,** potato fields, long clover, standing beans, and the like, to bushy coverts and underwood among **tall timber,** and that it never takes to the tree. Like our quail, it must be hunted for and found in the open, and marked into, and followed up in its covert, whatever that may be.

" In like manner, English and American grouse-shooting may be regarded as identical, except that the former is practised on heathery mountains, the latter on grassy plains; and that pointers are preferable on the latter, owing to the drought and want of water, and to a particular kind of prickly burr, which terribly afflicts the long-haired setter. The same qualities and performances constitute the excellence of dogs for either sport, and, as there the moors, so here the prairies, are, beyond all doubt, the true field for carrying the art of dog-breaking to perfection.

"To pheasant-shooting we have nothing perfectly

anal█████ Indeed, the only sport█
Amer████████ch at all resembles it, is r█
shoot█████ere they abound sufficien█
it wo█████e sportsman's while to p█
alone.█████ere they do so, there is·ne█
in the█████e of pursuing the two bir█
dissim█████hey may be in their other█
peculi████

"B█████ these facts in mind, the█
sports█████ill have no difficulty in █
the r█████en in the admirable work█
and t█████merican dog-breaker can█
mean█████ce so perfect an animal f█
with s█████e distress to himself or his█

Th█████ *Laws* for the State of N█
revise█████he Legislature in 1869, █
trodu█████ an Appendix

ADDRESS.

BROTHER SPORTSMEN,

There are many treatises on shooting (most, if not all, of which I have read) ; yet, in my humble opinion, the subject has never been half fathomed.

In this little work I have endeavored to strike at the very roots of the sport, and to give a thorough explanation of the principles of the art of shooting ; and then to lead my pupils on, step by step, to the summit of the science, in the hope of teaching them to hit, with unerring certainty, swiftly flying objects ; and also to cure defects in bad marksmen, and make them good shots.

The subject of wild-fowl Shooting is purposely excluded ; not for the reason that I am less familiar with it than with other sports with dog and gun, but because, to do it justice would fill a volume ; and such having recently issued from the press, in the shape

1*

of a   lete and elabo

" W   there is no nee

I   ccustomed to th

boy   to shooting in

cou   ne places wher

cute   efore, in its

now   blic, in plain

and   oncise as

exp

CONTENTS.

ILLUSTRATIONS.

.

THE DEAD SHOT.

"I can, I'll not the truth disguise,
  Myself kill bees and butterflies,
  While flying quick from flower to flower.
  Tomtits and sparrows, pippits, larks,
  Are all to me as easy marks."—W. WATT.

HE only can be called a " dead shot" who can bring
down, with unerring precision, an October or November partridge whenever it offers a fair chance ;
i. e., rises within certain range.   No matter what the
line of flight taken by the bird ; whether transverse,
curved, rectilineal, oblique, or otherwise, to . right
or left, and to or from the sportsman ; if there are
no obstructions, as trees or fences, the dead shot will
knock it down dead and bag it ; and no game is considered killed that is not bagged.

This definition, however, does not imply that every
partridge which rises within range must be killed, in

order to sustain the character of a "dead shot." If so rigorous a construction were put upon the explanation given, a "dead shot" would be a nonentity. A too sudden surprise, a slip or stumble, a rheumatic twinge, or some other unexpected occurrence, may cause the best shot to miss. But, making allowances for all such events, with preparation and expectation at his elbow, few indeed are the "fair chances" that escape a dead shot.

Where game is abundant, and there is no scarcity of powder and shot, a great many birds may be killed in a day, by a very ordinary marksman; but he who, with few birds and few shots, fills the game-bag, is, at least, "a sportsman," if not "a dead shot."

An experienced sportsman may be compared with an experienced lawyer; the one is a man of few shots, but they always hit; the other of few words, but they are always to the point.

GUNS.

A HISTORY of the art of gun-making, with an account of all the varieties in sporting fire-arms, requires a volume of itself; even an epitome of the subject would extend these pages far beyond their proposed limits. And such a book, to be of any value as an authority, must have been written by a gun-maker of long experience. A sportsman, however, will shoot no better from reading an elaborate treatise on the art of welding and making guns and gun-metal. Such is the old-fashioned style of teaching young sportsmen how to shoot; or rather of filling out a volume on guns and shooting, which generally winds up with some fifty or sixty pages on the game laws; the latter being merely a reprint from "Burn's Justice." But these are subjects foreign to the purpose of "The Dead Shot." I will, therefore, only refer such of my readers who may wish to pursue very deeply the subject of gun-making, to Mr. Green-

er's admirable work on gunnery. Mr. Greener has
been a gunmaker from his youth, and has made the
art his study through life ; he is, therefore, an authority upon the subject. And as to the game laws, I recommend no books upon that subject except those
written by lawyers.

I shall now confine my remarks on Guns, to such
subjects only as are considered essential for the purposes of this volume.

Some men are extremely fastidious in regard to
guns; and where money is no great object to them,
they spend it freely with the gunmakers, who delight
in such customers, and greet their ears with all sorts
of flattery, such as—"I see, sir, you are a sportsman,
or you would not have made so judicious a remark."
"Really, sir, it is quite a pleasure to show you a
gun, because I find by your observations that you
know a good article when you see one." "None but
a sportsman would have made such a remark as that,
sir ; I therefore feel a confidence in recommending
that gun to you." "I saw, sir, the moment you handled it, that you knew how to use it; and unless I
am very much mistaken, sir, looking at your eye,
you are a dead shot; if not, that's the gun to make
you one."

Such is but a fair sample of the everyday blarney of gunmakers, both in town and country. Among my acquaintances is a sportsman, who from boyhood has had plenty of money at command; and who, when learning to shoot, was constantly changing his guns, and having new ones made to order; but after all he never became a " dead shot," and only shot tolerably well when forty years of age.

It is amusing to hear, in one's travels in remote districts, of the wonderful qualities of some extraordinary gun; generally an old-fashioned family relic, of fifty years old and upwards, as the " best killing gun in the whole neighborhood;" its possessor declaring that it will throw the shot stronger and farther than any modern gun of its size; but on testing, it is generally found inferior in every respect to modern guns of less than half its weight.

ADVICE IN THE SELECTION OF A GUN.

Beware of cheap guns! they are made of doubtful metal, termed " sham damn skelp," which is composed of the most inferior scrap iron. Though they may last a long time with care, and loading with

small charges, still they may be easily burst on increasing the charge.

The itinerant hardwaremen, or "cheap Jacks,"
pay from 15s. to 1l. each for "sham damn" guns ; and
sell them by "Dutch auction" in country market-
towns and villages, to small farmers and other un-
wary ones, at prices varying from 1l. 5s. to 2l. each.
Let all sportsmen and others who value life and limb,
beware of these, and indeed of all cheap guns. It is
impossible that a gun of good quality can be made
for double or even treble the price at which the
"sham damn guns" are sold.

With regard to the quality of the gun-metal, Mr.
Greener recommends those barrels which are possessed of the greatest degree of elasticity and tenacity
combined, and which will throw the shot strongest
and closest with the least artificial friction.

Opinions are conflicting as to the "mounting" of
the gun, *i. e.*, the length and bend of the gun-stock.
It is obvious, however, that these must be in proportion with the stature, and length of neck and arms of
the person for whom the gun is intended ; if the stock
be too straight, the sportsman will be apt to shoot
too high. A gun-stock that is long and much bent
(or crooked), is, in gunmaker's phraseology, "high-

mounted;" whereas one that is short, and nearly straight, is "low-mounted." A sportsman having short arms and a short neck, requires a low-mounted gun, and *vice versa*. It is, assuredly, a very important element in the gun, that it be proportionally mounted to the shooter's arms, neck, and shoulder, or it cannot always be brought up quickly and truly to his eye.

The gun that comes up to the shoulder and the eye with most ease and accuracy, is the one with which the shooter will do most execution. Most gunmakers now use a stock-gauge, by which they are enabled to fit the sportman's neck and arms to a nicety; though some makers, through not clearly understanding the use of the stock-gauge, say they prefer measuring a gentleman's neck and arms without one.

Do not select a gun with a long barrel. The sight-piece at the muzzle should not be large; the merest bright speck will be sufficient. Many sportsmen pay no regard to the sight-piece in shooting, and knock it off purposely; but this is wrong, for it is of essential service sometimes, particularly on making a shot by twilight, or when the sun is shining full in the face, or when taking aim at a sitting object; therefore no gun should be without a sight-piece.

2

The elevation of the rib which divides the barrel is, with some sportsmen, an object of first importance: because, in proportion to the elevation of the rib at the breech end of the barrel, so the gun throws the shot above the horizontal line of aim.

The young sportsman will do well to avoid using "low-shooting guns;" i. e., those which throw the centre of the shot under the visual line of aim. Guns of this defective construction are old-fashioned, and seldom met with at the present day, except in ancient flint-guns, which have now become mere objects of curiosity.

The remedy consists chiefly in the barrels of the gun being provided with an elevated rib, or made stout and thick at the breech end; but gradually tapering to the muzzle, where they should be thin as a silver threepenny current coin of the realm.

The locks are also a most important consideration in the choice of a gun. Select the best workmanship, and you will then have locks of fine quick action,—a highly desirable feature in a good gun.

A gun of larger calibre than is ordinarily used may, truly, be more effective in the hands of a sportsman, by reason of its carrying a heavier charge; but it is unsportsmanlike to use such a gun for partridge or pheasant shooting; though for grouse, black game, wild-fowl, and birds of large size, and extra strength and plumage, it is the legitimate weapon.

There is no doubt but weighty guns of large calibre have a considerable advantage over light ones of small gauge; but he who uses a large gun, capable of throwing a large charge of shot, must be prepared to carry without murmuring the additional weight of metal which of necessity exists in the larger gun; he must also carry more ammunition.

I am no advocate for very light guns: on the contrary, I consider it a defect, rather than improvement in the manufacture of fire-arms, to strive to produce a gun of the lightest weight. By lessening the weight of the piece the recoil is increased; and, if it could be supposed possible for a gun to be so constructed that it be no heavier than the charge or missile, as a natural result, and according to the laws of explosive force, on ignition of the powder, the missile and gun would each fly in opposite directions, with equal velocity.

The weight of the gun, however, is, to some men, of vast importance in a day's shooting, especially in a hilly country; and on that account, if for no other, many sportsmen prefer as light a gun as is consistent with safety.

For partridge shooting, the gun should not be of larger gauge than No. 12, nor of smaller than No. 16. As much execution may be done with a No. 14 as with a No. 13 ; the difference in the shooting being so trivial as to be imperceptible; but in *two* sizes larger or smaller, the extra strength of the one prevails over the other.

For grouse and black game shooting, the gun should be from No. 11 to No. 14 calibre ; using the smaller size at the commencement of the season, and the larger as soon as the birds become strong on the wing and wary.

THE SPORTSMAN'S GUN-PROOF.

All sportsmen, who have never done so, should try their guns by firing with different charges and different sized shot, at large sheets and quires of paper or pasteboard, set up at various measured ranges : the most effective range of the gun may thus be discovered, together with the most suitable charges of powder and shot. Notes should be made in writing at each discharge, by carefully examining the paper or pasteboard, not only as to the indentation, or number of pellets or shot-grains which hit the paper within a certain circumference, but also as to the penetration, or force of the shot through the pasteboard.

Experiments of the kind judiciously made and cautiously noted, will be found of great assistance to the sportsman as to the strength and capacity of his gun; and well worth the trifling expense of half a pound or so of gunpowder and a few quires of large coarse paper and pasteboard; the cost of these, and the few hours which must be attentively bestowed upon the practice, will be amply repaid to the sportsman, in the shape of many an extra brace of birds, with much valuable experience. Those who make these experiments find, to their astonishment, that they have hitherto been in error and ignorance as to the best range, and most killing charge for their guns.

Young sportsmen may be assured, that on proving their guns in this way themselves, they will find experience and personal observation, under these tests, are splendid instructors.

A very interesting and excellent mode of testing the shooting of a marksman, together with the elevation of his gun, may be had by repairing to the banks of a large pond, on a perfectly calm day, when the surface is like a mirror, and firing at objects at estimated distances; the sportsman can then see whether the shot strikes according to his aim; and he will generally find, that, to hit an object, as a stump or a floating cork or bottle at forty or fifty yards, he must aim above or beyond it.

On trying experiments of this kind, an observer should be placed on the right or left hand side of the pond; in which position he would be enabled to take more accurate observations than yourself; and could tell you to a few inches how far short or beyond the mark your shot strikes.

This experiment, however, is not so good as the one suggested at quires of thick paper; because it does not prove the penetration.

TECHNICAL NAMES RELATING TO THE PARTS OF A GUN.

Ante-chamber: the cavity which connects the hollow of the nipple with the chamber in the breech.

Bolt: the sliding piece which secures the barrels to the stock.

Breech : the piece containing the chamber which screws into the barrel.

Butt end of gun-stock: the broad end which is placed to the shoulder.

Cap of ramrod : the brass piece which encases the worm.

Chamber : the cavity of the breech in which the powder is deposited and exploded.

False-breech : the iron piece on the gun-stock which receives the breech-claws, and assists in holding the barrel firmly to the stock.

Elevated-rib : the raised metal along the upper surface between the two barrels.

Guard : the scroll of metal which defends the triggers.

Heel-plate : the iron or brass plate with which the butt-end of the stock is shod.

Loop : the clasp on the barrel, through which the bolt passes and secures it to the stock.

Nipple : the small perforated tube on which the cap is placed, and through which communication is formed with the powder in the chamber.

Nipple-wrench : a small instrument for screwing and unscrewing the nipples to and from the barrels.

Pipes : small pieces of tube by which the ramrod is held to the barrel.

Rib (upper and under): the longitudinal centre piece which unites the barrels and holds them together.

Side-nail : the screw which fastens the locks to the stock.

Sight-piece (in rifles called *sight-plate*): the little silver knob at the muzzle-end of the barrels.

Trigger-plate : the iron plate in which the triggers work.

Worm : the screw at the end of the ramrod.

TECHNICAL NAMES RELATING TO THE PARTS OF GUNLOCKS.

Bridle : the piece which caps the tumbler, and by aid of three screws holds various parts of the lock together.

Chain or swivel : the small swivel which connects the tumbler with the main-spring.

Cock (also called both hammer and striker): the movable piece outside the lock; which, on the trigger being pulled, strikes the nipple and explodes the cap.

Hammer: see " Cock."

Lock-plate: the flat surface forming the outside of the lock, and to the inside of which the small parts of the lock are screwed.

Main-spring: the larger steel spring by which the cock or hammer is made to strike the cap and explode it.

Scear: the piece which catches the tumbler, on the hammer being moved to half or full cock.

Scear-spring: the small spring which holds the scear in the notches of the tumbler at full or half cock.

Spring-cramp: a most useful little instrument for taking off and replacing the main spring of a gunlock.

Tumbler: the movable centre piece subservient to the cock and trigger.

Tumbler-screw: the outside screw which secures the cock or hammer to the tumbler.

GUNLOCKS.

In order to clean a gunlock it is necessary to take it to pieces—an exceedingly simple process, with which every sportsman should be acquainted. The only tools requisite for the purpose are, a spring-cramp and a small screw-driver.

2*

TO TAKE A GUNLOCK TO PIECES.

The first thing to be done is, to cramp and remove the main-spring: to do which, raise the hammer to full cock: apply the spring-cramp, and carefully screw it up till the hammer is powerless (one or two turns of the screw will be sufficient), press the scear and let down the hammer, and the main-spring may be taken off in the claws of the spring-cramp.

The other parts of the lock may all be taken off by merely turning out the screws; beyond which no force whatever need be used. Let the scear-spring be the last piece to be taken off; place the screws on a newspaper beside the parts they belong to, in order that there be no mistake.

TO PUT THE LOCK TOGETHER AGAIN.

First screw on the scear-spring, then the scear; then put in the tumbler; then the bridle; and after these are all in their places, put on the hammer and let it down. The main-spring may then be replaced: first cramp it with the spring-cramp, then hook it on the swivel, and slip the pivot into its berth; then take off the cramp, and the lock is ready for action.

In all these operations, remember, that no force whatever should be used, except in cramping the main-spring; and that must be done cautiously with the spring-cramp.*

In cleaning gunlocks, brush away all adhering substances out of the joints, holes, and crevices; rub up each piece separately with soft wash-leather, and be careful that no dampness, breathing, or perspiration be left upon them. Oil the pivot-nail or centre-piece of the tumbler, and the pivot of the scear; and be careful to use the finest oil, such as is purified expressly for watchmakers and gunsmiths.

If the gun be used on a wet or foggy day, the locks should be taken off and cleaned immediately afterwards.

* I am very much surprised to find that Col. Hawker, in every edition of his work on Guns and Shooting, gives erroneous instructions both for taking to pieces and putting together gunlocks. He directs the tumbler and hammer to be put on first, in putting a lock together, which is wrong; and then he gives directions as to a forcible pressure being necessary for putting on the scear and scear-spring; whereas no forcible pressure of any kind is necessary, as any one will find if he acts upon the instructions I have given above; and to the accuracy and expediency of which I pledge my reputation.

,

DISADVANTAGES OF A FOUL GUN.

When a gun is foul and dirty inside, it "kicks" with much more deviltry than when clean ; because of the increased friction and difficulty of forcing the charge. A gun that is damp or greasy inside, though in other respects perfectly clean, kicks violently, by reason of the moisture creating resistance.

A gun that has been carelessly put away, or long neglected, must not be expected to shoot so well or last so long as one which has received all proper and necessary attention.

The gun should be kept as clean and lubricous inside, or cleaner and smoother, if possible, than polished stone or steel ; and it will shoot so much the better.

Mr. Greener points out the advantages of an inside polish to the gun-barrels, when he says :—

"The science of the question may now be regarded as clearly established. Gun-barrels of the utmost tenacity, with insides of a cylindrical form, as true as possible, polished as fine as a mirror, with a moderate weight of shot calculated to suit the gun, and a good charge of granulated gunpowder, will give the greatest killing power, with the greatest amount of comfort, or absence of recoil, that is to be found in the pursuit of shooting."

When guns are used on salt-water or by the sea-side, they require great attention, both to the inside and outside the barrels; or they may very soon become injured. Oil must be employed freely, immediately after wiping them thoroughly dry on returning home; and the oil should be always wiped off before taking the gun out again.

Guns, when not in use, should be often looked to, wiped, and re-oiled with clean, fresh-oiled flannel or lint, free from all manner of dampness or heat; and the hands should be free from moisture or perspiration during the process, which if performed with gloves on, so much the better.

TO CLEAN THE GUN.

Sportsmen should take care that their guns are not neglected; they very soon become damaged; and if long laid by in a damp or dirty state, they sometimes receive irreparable and ruinous injury. It should not be forgotten that they are made of a metal which corrodes and rusts by neglect or damp; but with care and attention may be kept bright and clean as if fresh from the gunmaker's. Remember also, that few servants can be trusted at all times: and inside rust cannot be seen. Generally speaking, after a day's shooting, a gun requires cleaning: but if pure gunpowder and greased felt waddings are used in loading, these will be found to prevent accumulation of foulness in the barrel.

The only tools required for taking a gun to pieces and cleaning it, are a turnscrew, a nipple-wrench, and a cleaning rod.

Use cold water first, in washing out the gun after shooting: then finish the washing with hot water, not boiling hot, but just as hot as the hand can bear.

Do not force the water through the nipples longer or more than necessary; but, having removed all the foulness, wipe with cloth or tow; and as the barrels dry, wind fresh pieces of the cloth or tow on the cleaning rod, so as to fit tightly in the barrel; and then by rapidly forcing it up and down, the suction and expulsion of air quickly dries the barrels. Wipe them thoroughly dry both inside and outside; and do it quickly, or the rust will soon appear.

Be careful to leave no particle of tow in the chamber of the gun. Serious accidents have occurred through small pieces of tow being left sticking in the chamber.

The accident occurs on re-loading immediately after the first discharge; when, a small particle of ignited tow being left in the chamber of the gun, on tossing in the powder to reload, it instantly ignites, blowing off the sportsman's hand, or producing some such fearful result. Patent powder-flasks may now be had, which guard, in a great measure, against the serious effects of accidents arising from such a cause.

Occasionally unscrew and take out the nipples of the gun, to see that there is no rust or corrosive substance inside; but this need not be done on every occasion of cleaning the gun. Always turn them in again with oil.

The brass wire brush may be used now and then for removing the accumulations of "leading"—that metallic corrosion which, after much shooting, adheres to the barrels, inside, just above the spot where the charge lies.

But this process, it must be remembered, should only be performed when the gun is perfectly clean and dry inside. The steel brush is apt to scratch and injure the barrels, therefore the brass brush is preferable.

If the barrels become rusty inside through long neglect, of course they receive injury. In such an event, a piece of *very fine* emery paper should be used for scouring them; this may be done by winding some tow round the cleaning rod so as to fit tightly into the barrel, then roll the emery paper round the tow, and secure it with fine thread. When judiciously employed, this process, on being repeated a few times, removes all rust, and polishes and smooths the insides of the barrels to great advantage.

Use none but the finest emery paper that is made.

EXPERIMENTS IN LOADING.

One of the secrets of success in the book of a "dead shot" is the art of loading the gun with the most effective charge; and, simple as the process may appear to a bad shot, there are very many sportsmen who do not do their guns justice; they will not take the trouble to try them sufficiently at a mark, but rely on what the gunmaker states to be a proper charge, and which is seldom the correct one. The sportsman should test the gun himself, and discover by practical means the most deadly charge: and

THE LOADING POSITION.

there is no doubt but he may acquire a better knowledge of the power and range of his gun, with the most effective mode of charging it, by a few hours' practice at pasteboards and quires of large stout paper (*vide* pages 28–30), than by many months' practice at game in open country.

The proper quantum of powder in a charge varies according to the gun: some guns require more, some less, though of the same size and gauge.

The only correct mode of discovering the best and most killing charge of powder for any particular gun is, by firing with carefully weighed charges at a mark placed at a measured distance.

There have been great improvements of late years in the manufacture of gunpowder: the sportsman should never use an inferior quality; the best is very much stronger and purer, and does not foul the gun so quickly as the common sort.

Much diversity of opinion exists as to the size of shot best adapted for different species of game; but in these things practice is the best instructor. I shall, however, in the following pages state my opinion upon the subject, after years of experience. The sportsman ought always to be able to decide for himself as to the proper size of shot; taking into consideration the time of year, and the size of the bird he goes in pursuit of.

It is an error to use mixed shot, or those of various sizes mixed together; a charge of mixed shot is not so effective as one in which they are all of a size.

An overcharge of shot in a small barrel, rests too high in the cylinder; and being heavier than is strictly in accordance with the rules of gun-loading, the powder has not sufficient power to drive it with that force which is requisite; and which constitutes the most important element in strong and effective shooting.

Many birds are missed at long distances (though the aim be perfectly correct) through disproportionate and injudicious loading.

The fault generally consists in that of using too much shot, or too little powder; or it may be the size of the shot is too large for the object.

Old sportsmen always use more powder and less shot than young ones; the latter are so afraid they should not have enough shot in the gun to kill the object: and they sometimes erroneously fancy, when they miss, that the shot used is of too small a size.

An overcharge of powder is one of the chief causes of scattering the shot too much; and an overcharge of shot produces similar results, in addition to causing the gun to kick severely.

The smaller the shot the closer they lie in the barrel; and though large shot kills farther than small, if it hits, it is not desirable to use large shot except for large objects: because of the greater spread and the smaller number of pellets.

For instance, the chances are six to one against killing a sparrow, either sitting or flying, at thirty yards with No. 4 shot; whereas, with the same gun, at the same distance, a sparrow may be killed with certainty, either sitting or flying, with No. 10 shot.

These experiments, which appear so clear and simple, and may be so easily tested, are nevertheless either disregarded through ignorance, or disbelieved through a want of careful natural reflection, by young sportsmen: the consequence is, that ofttimes when their aim has been perfectly right, and they might have killed had they used shot of a proportionate size, the bird has flown away uninjured; having escaped being hit, though the charge flew all around it; but the shot being so large and few, not one happened to strike, or at all events not in a vital part.

It should be remembered, that on the instant of

force being applied to the shot, through the ignition of the powder, it is the undermost shot which propel the uppermost; and, all being solid globular particles, the force is not exactly central upon each shot; as it might be if they were in the shape of short pieces of tobacco-pipe placed one behind the other in regular layers: but the shot being perfectly round, a great many must necessarily receive their propellant power at the sides and otherwise than central; and so the flight of a few only of the shot goes direct to the centre of the mark.

To illustrate this proposition, let a man load a rifle with two bullets, both of which are much smaller in diameter than the gauge of the rifle : let the bullets lie one on the top of the other in the barrel; a wadding being placed over them to prevent their rolling out on taking aim. With a rifle so loaded, let one of the most experienced rifle-shots fire at a three-foot-target at sixty or a hundred yards; and the chances are very many against either bullet striking it. The reason is clear: the pressure, or force of the gunpowder, acting on the undermost bullet, presses the upper one out of its straight course; so that immediately on leaving the barrel, the uppermost bullet is forced aside, or out of its trajectory course; and at fifty or sixty yards, the two bullets are probably two, three, or six yards apart.

The same principle applies to large shot in a small barrel; though, of course, as the size of the shot is diminished, so the deviation from the true line is decreased. Sportsmen who wish to pursue and look more strictly into this theory, should procure a few inches of small glass tube, of the same interior size as the barrels of their guns: plug one end of the tube, and put in a charge of large shot; it will then be seen how they lie, one above the other, in the gun; the vacua between them being many, and large, so that the pressure upon each shot cannot be central; therefore, on being forced out of the gun, there must be a tendency to diverge. If then he takes another tube, and introduces a charge of small shot, he will see that those lie more evenly and compactly; and consequently, on being forced out of the barrel, the divergency must be very much less.

After years of experience and a careful study of the subject, theoretically and practically, I recommend :—

For partridge shooting during the first fortnight in September, No. 7 shot; then No. 6 to the middle of October; and afterwards No. 5 to the end of the season.

For pheasant shooting, No. 6 in October; No. 5 during the rest of the season.

For grouse, No. 7 the first fortnight, then No. 6; and, when very wild, No. 5.

For black game, No. 6 at first; No. 5 in October; then No. 4 to the end of the season. If a larger gun than common be used, larger shot will be required, and so much the better for black game, when wild.

For woodcock use No. 7 or No. 6.

For snipes No. 8 is best; but larger than No. 7 should never be used.

For shooting wild ducks with a shoulder gun, use No. 5, 4, or 3, according to the size of the gun. When boat-guns, stanchion-guns, or punt-guns are used, very much larger shot will be required.

When game is very wild, cartridges may be used with considerable advantage; but they should not be made with larger shot than those recommended for the different species above enumerated.

It is a common practice among prize shooters to arrange loose stringy pieces of tow among the shot, or to wrap the charge in paper, in order to prevent the shot scattering; but unless very judiciously performed, no extra advantage is gained by such experiments.

A thirteen-gauge gun, which is perhaps the most usual size for partridge and general shooting, should be charged liberally with powder, according to the strength and quality of the barrels: but 1¼ oz. of shot is the very utmost that should be used in a single charge; from 1 oz. to 1¼ oz. will generally be found the most effective charge: and the highest average execution will be done at partridge shooting with No. 6 shot.

For a gun of No. 16 gauge use a liberal charge of powder, and 1 oz. shot at the most; if one-eighth less than an oz., probably the gun will throw it stronger. No. 7 is the most killing sized shot for a gun of this caliber.

Mr. Greener, in his book on Gunnery, makes the following observations; which it will be seen very nearly coincide with my views upon the same subject :—

" From many experiments I am inclined to think that a fourteen-gauge, two feet eight inches barrel, should never be loaded with above 1¼ oz. of shot (No. 6 will suit best), and the utmost powder she will burn. A fifteen-gauge will not require more than 1 oz. : and no doubt No. 7 would be thrown by her quite as strong as No. 6 by the fourteen-gauge gun, and do as much execution at forty yards, with less recoil"

In loading large guns, and indeed all guns, due attention must always be paid to the quality of the metal of which the gun is composed, as well as the size of the barrels ; and the charge must be regulated accordingly: the better the metal the more freely the powder may be used.

The best waddings for loading sporting guns are made of felt, the edges of which should be anointed with oil.

In all guns a good firm wadding should be placed over the powder; a slight one will suffice for the shot. In proportion with the size of the gun, the thickness of the wadding should be increased.

BREECH-LOADERS.

The invention of breech-loading guns is not by any means a new discovery; it was tried in various forms, by scores of inventors, soon after the introduction of fire-arms. Subsequent inventors have from time to time, in years long past, frequently applied the most searching ingenuity to the subject; and though they succeeded in almost every case, in producing a breech-loader, in no one instance have they ever succeeded in making one possessing equal advantages to a muzzle-loader.

The modern inventions which have been patented of late years are similar to those which were experimentalized upon over and over again; and finally abandoned, because the inventors despaired of producing a perfect form of breech-loader, or one that would kill with equal force at equal distance to a muzzle-loader: and killing at long distances being the greatest desideratum in a sporting-gun, if the breech-loader fails in this respect it cannot be said to be equal to the other.

Great credit is due to inventors for having succeeded in producing a very handsome and useful gun for short ranges; but beyond that, no corresponding advantages are gained by present inventions.

The most strenuous advocates of the breech-loading system, as applied to guns, have failed in their attempts to prove that the advantages are equal to those possessed by the muzzle-loaders.

Breech-loading *rifles*, however, are among the most valuable improvements of the present age. They are quite as safe in the handling, and nearly as effective in range, as the muzzle-loaders. For mili-

3

tary purposes they are invaluable, especially to troops of cavalry; and to the hunter who treads the wild forests and jungles of eastern countries, or the western prairies of America, where successive instantaneous loading may sometimes save him his life, or double and treble his sport, there is no weapon on which he can so faithfully rely as the breech-loading rifle.

As regards breech-loading *guns*, they appear to be progressing towards perfection, but at present are certainly wide of the mark.

I have no wish to discourage those who possess breech-loaders; they will find them useful for every purpose but wet days and long shots. As regards myself, I use a breech-loader for tame game, and in early season; but for all purposes of wild game and real sport, long shots, and security at the breech, I give infinite preference to muzzle-loaders.

It is impossible there can be a more fatal argument against breech-loading guns than that they are of much weaker range and effect than muzzle-loaders. When that defect can be removed, and the breech-loader made to exceed, or even equal, the other in those most essential particulars, then, and not till then, will breech-loaders supersede muzzle-loaders.

Breech-loaders must be well made : one of inferior metal, or bad or careless workmanship, would be a most dangerous weapon.

The construction of a breech-loader will be found on examination to be exceedingly simple; the lever, the joint, and the bolt, being the chief parts in connection with the apparatus for loading at the breech.

The cartridges with which these guns are loaded contain the complete charge of powder, shot, and cap, all in one; together with a small pin which explodes the cap in the powder, on being struck by the hammer. Good and successful shooting with a breech-loader depends, in a great measure, on the care and attention with which the cartridges are made. They must fit the barrel closely, in order to shoot well; but if too closely, they are liable to be set fast in the barrel.

The chief advantages possessed by the breech-loading gun are these :—

1. The simplicity and quickness with which it may be loaded. And the risks incident to carelessness or negligence, in loading one barrel whilst the other is charged and capped, or at full cock, are entirely obviated in the breech-loader.

2. The ramrod, loading-rod, powder-flask, shot-pouch, and cap-holder, are all dispensed with.

3. Much of the time, trouble, risk, and waste of ammunition on drawing a charge are obviated; because the cartridge may be easily and quickly withdrawn from the breech-loader, by simply turning the lever and opening the joint.   Therefore there is no occasion to fire off the breech-loader at the close of a day's shooting; the charge may be simply drawn out of the barrel and returned to the cartridge pouch.

4. The breech-loader may also be charged in rapid succession, whilst the sportsman is lying on the ground, or in a cramped position.

5. The moisture, which it is said is sometimes forced down upon the powder by the wadding, from the sides of the barrel, is not disturbed; but the powder, in its purest state, is deposited at the breech-end of the barrels.

6. The barrels may be cleaned with much greater facility than those of a muzzle-loader.

In addition to these, it may also be stated that there are some other minor advantages which should not be overlooked.   For some purposes of sport it is sometimes desirable, when in the field, to change the shot as quickly as possible: for instance, when snipe-shooting, it is not unusual to fall in with wild duck or teal; when, if the sportsman is enabled to mark them down, or discover them before they rise, he proceeds to extract the snipe-shot, and load with No. 4, or a cartridge. With a breech-loader the risk and trouble of drawing the charge at the muzzle are avoided ; and the cartridge containing snipe-shot may be withdrawn in a moment, and replaced with one containing large shot. And then, should the sportsman fail in his attempts to stalk the wild fowl, the cartridges may be changed again with the same facility ; whereas, similar circumstances with a muzzle-loader would necessitate the trouble and risk of twice drawing, changing, and replacing the shot. In the hands of careless, over-anxious, excitable, and nervous sportsmen, a breech-loader is, perhaps, the safer gun of the two ; because all the risks incident to loading are avoided. Carelessness, nervousness, haste, or over-anxiety in loading, would scarcely incur danger with the breech-loader ; whereas, in the muzzle-loader, they are the causes of many accidents.

On entering a house with a muzzle-loader, or riding or driving along the road, it is usual to insist on the *caps* being removed from the nipples. With the breech-loader the *whole charge* may be as quickly withdrawn, and the gun is then comparatively harmless.

The disadvantages are these:

1. The breech-loader does not shoot so strong, nor kill so far as the muzzle-loader, though allowed a quarter of a drachm of powder extra.

2. The breech-loader is of· necessity much heavier than a muzzle-loader of the same gauge.

3. It is more expensive as regards ammunition, and also as to the gun itself; the latter by reason of its not lasting so long, and its greater liability to get out of repair than a muzzle-loader.

4. The recoil on discharge is heavier, and the report louder than that produced by a muzzle-loader.

5. The penetration of wet and damp, in rains, fogs, or mists, between the false-breech and barrels, and often into the cartridge itself, cannot be avoided in the present form of breech-loader; more especially in one that has been much used. And if the cartridge-case gets damp it adheres to the barrel, and cannot be removed without considerable difficulty.

6. There is obviously a greater risk of bursting: indeed, the safety of the breech-loader, after much usage, becomes doubtful, by reason of the escape of gas between the false-breech and barrels; particularly after the trying vibrations of heavy charges.

7. The time and trouble required in filling the

cartridges, and the danger attending that operation, before going out shooting, are very considerable ; and it is with one peculiar form of cartridges only that the breech-loader can be used; and if purchased of the gun-maker ready filled, they come very expensive.

8. The operation of making and filling the cartridges is, to a sportsman, a tedious, dirty, dangerous, and laborious one ; quite as much so as making fireworks.

9. Another serious objection to the breech-loader is, the great weight of ammunition that must be carried, in the shape of ready-made cartridges, when going to the Highlands or any remote shooting quarters.   And then arises the difficulty of keeping them perfectly dry in damp weather ; and every one knows how very soon the damp will penetrate through a paper case, and cake and weaken the force of the gunpowder.

10. The cartridges must be carried in a strong case, with divisional compartments for each cartridge.   In the event of their being carried loose they become damaged ; and the danger of so carrying them is excessive, by reason of the results which may ensue in the event of a fall or accident in getting over a hedge or otherwise, whereby a blow or fric-

tion is given to the metal pin which explodes the cap.

11. The extra weight incurred in being obliged to carry a sufficient number of cartridges for a day's sport, in a very cumbersome leather case, with iron compartments, considerably exceeds the ordinary weight of powder-flask and shot-pouch, with ammunition for a similar amount of sport.

12. Another of the principal defects in the breech-loader is the flat surface of the breech ; which scientific and practical experimenters have proved to be erroneous, by reason of the much greater power and extra force which may be obtained from the conical interior form of solid breech : the rule being, that "force cannot be expended and retained also :" and, as it must of necessity be expended to a certain degree by explosion and recoil on a flat-surfaced breech, extra powder is required to produce like effects to those which result from the solid conical breech. The recoil is also considerably greater on a flat surface than on a tapering one.

13. Joints, joinings, slides, and bolts, are all inferior to a well-made screw, as regards soundness of the breech. A perfectly solid breech, free from all suspicious joinings, crevices, and openings, *must be*

by far the safer and more effective one in any instrument in which so searching a substance as gunpowder has to be compressed and exploded.

Among the minor disadvantages are these :

On reloading, it is necessary to draw out the case of the discharged cartridge before inserting a full one. It is true, the discharged cartridge may generally be withdrawn almost instantly; but, if intended to be refilled and used again another day, it must be carefully replaced in the cartridge-case, in one of the divisional compartments; for if carried loose in the pocket it is soon spoilt. Therefore, if these important minutiæ be taken into consideration, it will be found, after all, that there is but very little saving of time in re-charging the breech-loader.

With regard to re-filling the cartridge-cases, the makers warrant that the discharged cases may be refilled and used again with the same facility and effect, some of them two or three times. This, however, is not always so; on the contrary, the cases expand so much on explosion of the powder, that, when re-filled, they are sometimes not only difficult to thrust into the barrel, but, on second explosion, they stick so fast, that in many instances the copper end comes off, on the case being attempted to be withdrawn; and the paper is left inside. And then, unless a loading-rod is at hand, with which to force out the paper-case, your breech-loader is powerless.

None but those who have experienced the difficulty of extracting a bursted cartridge-case, which adheres firmly to the sides of the barrel, can imagine the annoyance it causes : and if the cases get damp, or if re-filled ones are used, the difficulty is constantly occurring. And then the "extractor" is of little use beyond pulling away the brass bottom of the cartridge, and leaving the paper case the more difficult to remove.

Unless the brass pin which explodes the cap is made very precisely, a mis-fire is inevitable. If there is any corrosive substance upon it, or upon the sides of the hollow in which it travels, the hammer will fail to drive it home, or explode the cap. The hammer must strike it in exact position, or the pin will bend ; any extra length or protrusion of the pin, or any dampness or foulness which causes it to stick, or if the pin be nipped in any way so as to weaken the force of the hammer, a mis-fire will probably be the result. And the pins must not be too loose, or they will drop out of the cartridges on any sudden or violent exertion on the part of the sportsman.

If on drawing out an unexploded cartridge, the brass end comes off, or breaks away from the paper-case, it will not be advisable to use the cartridge in that state : it cannot be safe to explode it in the barrel of a breech-loading gun ; in fact, it would be almost as unsafe as a loose charge of powder. And in the event of the cap missing fire in a breech-loading cartridge, it is not desirable to recap the cartridge. When once the brass and the pasteboard part company, the power of retaining the explosive force within the case is considerably weakened, and so is the *expulsive* force.

The rapidity with which a succession of shots may be made, is urged as one of the chief recommendations of the breech-loader ; but rapidity of firing is seldom desirable : and the barrels may become heated to danger. The sportsman's every-day success frequently depends on the *range* of his gun ; but seldom on the rapidity of loading and firing it.

For partridge-shooting during the month of September, or at all events during the first fortnight, a safe and well-made breech-loading gun is a highly desirable one ; but later in the season, when partridges become wild and require hard hitting, a muzzle-loader is by far the more useful weapon.

The crowning feature in every gun is the force and effect with which it throws the shot: the gun which will throw the shot sharpest and strongest, and consequently killing the farthest, is, to all intents and purposes, the better gun in the hands of a good sportsman.

The following facts, the results of the latest public tests between breech-loaders and muzzle-loaders, are submitted to the impartial consideration of sportsmen; they are so clear that they need not a word in explanation, beyond this, that they took place publicly at Cremorne and Hornsey, in the years 1858 and 1859, in presence of several experienced sportsmen. Many guns were tried of the same caliber by various makers; the same sized shot were used on both sides, and the targets placed at precisely the same distances.

The following are fair average results selected from the score-sheet:

Breech-loader, charged with 3 drachms gunpowder and 1¼ oz. shot.

Muzzle-loader, charged with 2¾ drachms gunpowder and 1¼ oz. shot.

RESULTS.*

Breech-loader, 170 pellets in target: penetration 19 (measuring through 19 sheets of paper).

Muzzle-loader, 231 pellets in target: penetration 48 (measuring through 48 sheets of paper).

It is impossible for results to have been more conclusive, conducted as they were with great care and impartiality; and in presence of some of the most strenuous supporters of the breech-loading system.

Other trials took place at Ashburnham Park, and Kilburn Victoria Rifle ground, with similar results; the breech-loaders being signally beaten, despite their extra allowance of gunpowder.

The breech-loader *must* have its extra quarter drachm of powder; consequently, the barrels must be of stouter substance than the muzzle-loader of the same caliber; and yet, with both these extras, the shooting is not so strong as that of the other.

Undoubtedly, the most perfect and useful gun in the hands of a sportsman, is that which possesses the power of shooting strongest and farthest with the smallest charges.

* These results were publicly made known at the time, through the columns of every sporting paper in the land.

Bad shots, inexperienced sportsmen, and those who are ignorant of the true principles of good shooting, will probably be heard frequently express- ing their opinions in favor of the breech-loader; and probably with much honesty of purpose; for perhaps such men may find that they kill more game with a breech-loader than with a muzzle-loader.

Mr. Greener, who has written a very able book on Gunnery, and who has devoted his whole life to that subject, and obtained one or two patents for breech- loading guns, candidly admits that, in his opinion, there is no possibility of inventing a breech-loader such as would shoot with equal force and effect to that of a well-made muzzle-loader.

Mr. Greener's opinion on the subject is worthy of the highest consideration; he sums up his remarks in the following damnatory sentence: " Breech- loaders do not shoot nearly so well, and are not half so safe as muzzle-loading guns."

It has always been urged, on the part of the advo- cates of the breech-loading system, that for the pur- pose of a punt-gun for wild-fowl shooting, the breech-loader is invaluable, because it dispenses with the necessity, on re-loading, of shifting so heavy a gun to the aft part of a very fragile boat; this is undoubtedly an advantage; but then again, the great and insurmountable disadvantage *as to range*, stares us in the face. And for a punt-gun, of all things, range is the most important consideration. Wild-fowl are, by nature, so extremely vigilant; and the punter so exposed on the open water, without any screen to hide him, that the most skilful fowlers find it very difficult to approach within range: it is there-fore an indisputable fact, that the gun which shoots sharpest and farthest is, to all intents and purposes, the best and only serviceable one to the practical punter: and such a gun is not to be found among the breech-loading punt-guns.

A writer in a recent number of the Sporting Re-view says: "Having tested several of these novel-ties or breech-loading punt-guns side by side with muzzle-loaders, I maintain, *in defiance of every gun-maker in England*, that the breech-loading punt-gun has yet to be made that will equal a good sound per-cussion muzzle-loader, in range, compactness, and strength of throwing the shot. A muzzle-loader punt-gun will kill one-fourth farther than a breech-loader; and if the muzzle-loader be charged with a cartridge, it will beat the breech-loader nearly one-third."

RUDIMENTARY LESSONS.

"Enough! permit me now to sing
The art of killing birds on wing."—WATT.

THE young sportsman should commence by using
himself to handle and carry the gun in a safe position :
then point it at small objects, sitting, flying, and running fast and slow. When he has had several lessons on these, he may load with a little powder, but
no shot; and after firing away some two or three
dozen charges in course of a week, he may commence
by shooting small birds sitting, using very small shot,
and loading with small charges.

Shooting sparrows from a pigeon-trap is very good
initiatory practice for partridge-shooting ; and if a
very small portion of the tips of the feathers in each
wing be clipped off with a pair of scissors, or if a
portion of their tails be cut off in the same manner, it
will make them fly so steadily, and so much like

FIRING ATTITUDE NO. 2.

young partridges, that it will be as good practice as he can make, before the shooting season commences. Another mode of making sparrows fly steadily is, by slipping a bit of paper over their heads ; the process is performed by simply cutting a hole in the centre of a piece of paper about three or four inches square, and by putting their heads through it; the paper forms a collar, which impedes their flight considerably.

When the dog points at game, never run, but walk leisurely up, taking firm steps ; you will then have a better command of your range, and the flight of the bird when it rises (which it may do at any instant), than if loping along with hasty strides.

On presenting and taking aim, always remember that the hand which touches the trigger must obey the eye ; not the eye the hand.

Put your left hand forward in advance of the guard, to grasp the barrel and assist in holding the gun steady (see frontispiece).

Light guns may be held firmly, by placing the left hand in front of the trigger-guard (see opposite plate, and compare with the frontispiece) ; and a strong man can accustom himself to hold a tolerably heavy gun in this manner ; it is, however, a plan I do not advocate: all the good shots I ever met with, put their left hand forward in *advance* of the guard, as shown in the frontispiece; and such is the safer and better position.

A young sportsman always profits by going out with a good steady old shot, and learns more in a week, of the art of finding and approaching his game, than he would in a year with a bad shot.

Young sportsmen must not be vexed or disheartened at missing; generally speaking the reason why they miss is, because they shoot both behind and below the bird; the result of the trigger-finger not being quick enough in obeying the eye.

When you miss, always endeavor to ascertain the cause; and having discovered it, resolutely determine to profit by the experience gained, and sooner or later you will probably become a dead shot.

Young sportsmen should always prefer old dogs to young ones; and the less they talk to them the better they will hunt.

Don't "fluster" on going up to a dog at his point: if you do you must not expect to kill.

Never condescend to trespass or poach, nor poke your gun through a hedge, nor shoot birds on the ground.

Never pick up a shot bird, nor allow your dogs or attendant to do so, until you have re-loaded. And when in company with another sportsman, if he fires and kills a bird, halt immediately, and do not advance a step until he has re-loaded.

Two sportsmen shooting in company should each, in general, fire only at those birds the heads of which are pointed to that side of the beat on which he walks: at birds going straight away, each sportsman should take the best outside shot on his particular side.

Single birds, on getting up fairly in front of both sportsmen, should be taken alternately. But when a single bird rises in front of any individual sportsman, apart from his companion, the shot belongs exclusively to him on whose side the bird rose.

The necessity of observing strict silence when beating for partridges or grouse, cannot be too strictly impressed upon the minds of young sportsmen. The human voice, whether addressed to your companion or your dog, is sure to alarm the birds, if near enough to hear it.

Young sportsmen must not forget that birds have ears as well as eyes.

It is an indisputable fact, that thousands of young

sportsmen who so frequently miss the flying objects
of their aim, do so through shooting below them.
They are unable to give the reason themselves; whereas it is so clear, that reflection alone would tell them
the fact: gravity is always acting upon the shot, and
drawing it to the ground in its trajectory course
through the air; consequently the body of it strikes
below the horizontal line of the sportsman's aim.

Good shooting is sure to follow, if the young sportsman will only aim in advance of flying cross-shots,
and above straightforward ones.   There is no fear
of young sportsmen shooting too high or too far in
front; they are always too low and too point-blank
in their early practice.

Young sportsmen should be careful to carry the
gun at all times in a safe position; particularly when
walking or taking the field with another sportsman.
I know nothing more detrimental to good shooting
than to find the muzzle of your friend's double-barrel
constantly staring at you whenever you are walking
on a level with him, or happen to turn your head to
look after him.   An old sportsman, on noticing a
carelessness of the sort, would return home and refuse
to go out with a man who carried the muzzle of his
gun so low as to be always pointing toward his person.

In cocking or uncocking your gun, always keep the muzzle pointing in the air above the level of human heads.

On getting over a fence, grasp the gun in the left hand round the barrels, above the hammer and breech; the right hand being quite at liberty to lay hold of a bough or stake to assist you in climbing.

Young sportsmen, in general, reckon too much on their sport, and anticipate an unreasonable amount of success; they are, consequently, very often disappointed, especially grouse shooters: but this arises from the fabulous reports of large packs of grouse to which the tyro is to be introduced; so that nothing short of unprecedented success would fully realize his expectations. Such reports, as well as others (equally untrue) as to the astonishing numbers killed, generally proceed from those interested in the moors; or who have an ulterior or lurking design upon the purse of the English sportsman. These individuals, who reside chiefly beyond the banks of the Tweed, appear to utter falsehoods as if under the protection of a license. Let sportsmen beware of such characters.

The young sportsman's expectations on entering upon the shooting season, or a day's sport, should be moderate, never too sanguine; and then, if ill-success attends him, he will be the better able to bear the disappointment without disturbing his nerves in such a manner as to cause him to miss his shots at the latter part of the day.

Above all things, guard against a feeling of envy at the better success of your companion.

Three or four sportsmen in a party, are too many for sport; they should divide into two parties, and go on separate beats, by which arrangement they will bag more game, and incur less danger to themselves.

When a covey of partridges or a brood of grouse rises at your feet, do not put the gun to your shoulder immediately, and so keep aiming until they are forty yards off: a protracted aim is the cause of many a miss: rather look at the birds an instant, select one as your mark, and then deliberately level the gun and down with it: then instantly choose another for the other barrel; and being equally steady and accurate, you will drop that also.

In order to bag your game you must either hit it in a vital part or break a wing; and then it is either your own fault or that of your dog, if it is not brought to bag.

ERRORS OF YOUNG SPORTSMEN.

The reasons why young sportsmen miss fair shots have never been fully discussed, nor have any direct rules been laid down by which to ensure their hitting the object, at all times, when within range. The inconsiderate assert, that there are no rules which can be of any assistance to a student of the art of shooting flying objects. They might as well say the same of rifle practice, and naval and military gunnery; whereas in truth there are rudiments and aphorisms in the art of accurate shooting, which require as careful study and observance by the successful shot, as do the rules and principles applicable to any other art.

There are many practitioners who sometimes kill, though they often miss; but there are not many real proficients in the art; and few are enabled to explain the causes of missing, or to boast of being certain of hitting a flying bird at any distance within range, and in any line of flight.

The oldest and most highly reputed shots, though they shoot and kill, sometimes miss without being able to explain the reason; and often attribute it to the reverse of what it actually is.

I shall, therefore, endeavor to explain the principal causes of the young sportsman missing the flying object of his aim, and point out the fundamental rules of the art of accurate shooting.

A very great deal of the evil lies in the unequal length, breadth, or form of the gun-stock. Much more depends on this than many sportsmen are disposed to believe: indeed, more bad shooting arises from a disproportionately mounted gun than from any other cause. The length of the stock should be proportionate with the length of the sportsman's neck, and the reach of his arms. Gunmakers, in general, do not pay sufficient regard to these important minutiæ; but, disregarding the length of arms and neck of their customers, tall and short, fat and thin, long-necked and short-necked individuals, one and all have the same or indifferent lengths of gun-stocks. This, then, is a defect of much more importance to the young sportsman than many would suppose. Rifles, in particular, should have stocks of a length and bend to suit *exactly* the neck and arms of the man who uses them.

If the stock of a gun is too short, it is difficult to get it to the shoulder in correct position; and it is still more difficult to hold it firmly and steadily at

the shoulder so as to shoot accurately at a quickly
moving object. .

And if too long, the difficulty of getting it up instantly into exact position is increased; and it is then
very troublesome to take a faithful aim, the arms
being of necessity too far extended to be in an easy
position; and the neck has to be stretched painfully,
to bring the eye in line with the barrel.

A change of guns from day to day, from a stiff or
hard-pulling trigger to an easy-going one, may cause
the best shot to miss, unless he can constantly remember whether he has the stiff-going lock or the easy
one. The stock of one gun may be longer than the
other, or the barrels heavier; these, though apparently trifling circumstances, are sufficient to be the cause
of missing, in a man accustomed to a favorite or
particular sort of gun which exactly suits him.

Missing fair shots does not arise so much through
an imperfect knowledge of the use of the gun, as
from a want of confidence; or through fatigue, anxiety, or some such effect on the nervous system;
though it more frequently arises from the causes before
stated.

Young sportsmen miss more birds by shooting
under them than by any other error: they *will not*

4

shoot high enough; because they forget the very rudiments of the art, and that gravitation is acting upon
their shot all the way in its passage through the air.
By aiming point blank at the object, the shot must,
as a natural result, strike below it.   In proof of this,
let a sportsman aim point blank at a fixed object,
forty yards off; and unless the gun has an elevated
rib, the shot will be found to have struck below the
aim; and if this be so at a fixed object, the shot must
of necessity go very much farther beneath a rising or
flying one.   And when it is taken into consideration
that all birds of game generally continue rising (except
when flushed on a hill) whilst within reach of the
sportsman's gun, this may be stated as one of the
principal and indisputable reasons why young sportsmen miss.

Pheasants, for instance, gain fifteen or eighteen
inches in altitude, between the time of pulling trigger
and that of the shot reaching forty yards.   And partridges often quite as much ; therefore the centre of
the charge is too frequently thrown under the visual
line of aim, by reason alone that the sportsman makes
not sufficient allowance for the ascending motion of
the bird in its flight from, or across his aim.

The young sportsman should never expect or

think of killing, if, at the time of pulling trigger, he sees the bird on wing above the muzzle of the gun. Some guns, however, are specially sighted and constructed for throwing the shot nearly two feet above the aim at forty yards: this may be done by a very thick rib, high at the breech-end of the barrels, and tapering to nothing at the muzzle.

There are but few sportsmen in whom the fault of missing lies in their shooting too high or too forward: it is almost always the contrary.

It is astonishing how stubborn young sportsmen are to believe in the principle, that it is necessary to fire in advance of a distant flying object for the purpose of killing it: they persist in the foolish notion that almost on the instant of pulling trigger, the shot reaches the object aimed at. Many years ago I was one among that stubborn class, until convinced of my error in a simple but somewhat extraordinary manner; which I relate for the purpose of endeavoring to impress upon my readers the importance of this fundamental principle. I was out shooting one day, in the month of October, in a large turnip-field, with my dogs and gun, when a brace of partridges rose at the distance of fifty-five or sixty yards: they flew rapidly to the right, in direct line, one behind the other, at a space of about two feet apart. I took deliberate aim a few inches in advance of the leading bird, and fired; when, to my surprise, the hindmost bird fell dead, and the leading one, which was the object of my aim, flew untouched. At the moment I felt so astonished at the result, that I could not recover myself soon enough to discharge the other barrel at the bird which had flown away. On picking up my bird, I found five shots had struck it in the head and neck: so that my aim, which was at least two feet six inches in advance of the bird killed, was not any too much at the distance and rate at which they were flying. I felt so forcibly the erroneous principle upon which I had hitherto been shooting, and so delighted at the lucky but accidental discovery I had made of my own error, that I felt as if a curtain had risen before me, and exposed the true secrets of the art of killing cross shots. And I can truly assert, that this simple but singular discovery, did more towards improving me in the art of shooting, than all the advice and instruction I had received from practical and venerable sportsmen. Some of my sporting friends, shortly afterwards, on congratulating me on a " very sudden and wonderful improvement in my shooting at long ranges," inquir-

vation, they would, on reflection, see the necessity of making the suggested allowances for gravitation at long shots.

PRESSING VERSUS PULLING TRIGGER.

Professors of musketry tell us they never *pull* a trigger, but *press* it; and if that doctrine applies to rifle practice, surely it does also, with equal force, to gun-practice.

On reference to English dictionaries, I find "to pull" means to "draw violently, or forcibly;" and certainly no such violent or forcible means are required in putting the trigger of a gun in motion. I am therefore disposed to agree with the professors of musketry, that the term "pulling" is erroneous and inapplicable, with reference to the discharge of the rifle or the gun.

Certain it is, that he who can discharge his piece with the least possible motion of the hand, stands the best chance of hitting his mark.

In discharging the gun, the finger alone should act on the trigger; the hand is required for holding the gun firmly to the shoulder.

GRAVITATION.

It is impossible for any man to become a dead shot until he is familiar with the laws of gravitation. Simple and natural as those laws will appear on explanation and reflection, there are thousands of sportsmen who have erroneous ideas upon them. I have often been astonished at the ignorance in which I have found experienced sportsmen, on discussing the subject with them.

I have no hesitation in saying,—if a man ever hopes or expects to shoot well, he must have some knowledge of the fundamental principles of gravitation : he must remember that all material substances, on being forced through the air unsupported, incline towards the earth ; that is, keep dropping nearer and nearer to the ground as they proceed through the atmosphere. So also with shot, as it passes through the air, forcibly expelled by gunpowder ; and whether slowly or swiftly, it is influenced by the laws of gravitation, from the moment of its expulsion from the barrel, until its horizontal force is exhausted and it falls to the ground. The trajectory course of the shot is curvilinear ; consequently, if a straight barrel, of the same substance throughout, that is to say, as thick at the muzzle as it is at the breech, were fired in exact horizontal line with a distant object, the shot would strike considerably below it.

The reason why many young sportsmen kill flying objects with tolerable certainty when within short range, and miss those at long range, is because they always fire point blank at every thing, regardless of distance and other important considerations. When they kill, the objects are in fact so near that there is no perceptible declination of the shot, or not sufficient for the bird to escape all the strong shot; whereas, on the other hand, by taking the same point blank aim at more distant objects, they are missed through not allowing for declination, or gravity of the shot, and speed of the flying bird.

It is calculated that at forty yards the gravitation of the shot is four inches, and at sixty yards eight inches.

At the moment of taking aim, and levelling the gun point blank at the bird, the visual line is right, if the shot could be conveyed to the object instantaneously, and without being affected by the laws of gravitation. But such a thing is impossible, because, in addition to the declination of the shot, the trigger has to be

4*

pressed, and the shot has to travel the whole distance through the air between the gun and the bird; during which, the bird is all the while gradually rising, and the shot gradually falling; so that, by the time the shot reaches the end of the supposed visual line of aim, the distance below the object aimed at, and the hitting place of the shot, is several inches; and thus it is, through neglecting to consider carefully these simple principles, that young sportsmen shoot at flying objects and miss them.

It will, therefore, be seen that in taking aim at a flying object, the gun should not be held in such a manner that the visual line is upon a level with the bird: but, allowance must be made for the tendency of the shot to fall to the ground, for the rapid motion of the bird, and for the time which must elapse between pressing trigger and the shot hitting or reaching the object; consequently, the visual line of aim should be both above and in advance of the flying object, more or less, according to long or short range; the one to allow for gravitation of the shot, and the other for the space which the bird advances between the time the aim is taken, and the precise moment of the shot hitting it.

DEFLECTION.

By practising at a target in windy weather, the sportsman will soon learn the theory of deflection. Of course, the subject more materially affects rifle-practice; nevertheless, it is also an element for consideration in the art of shooting flying objects. The sportsman should place the target in an open field, so that the wind blows across or to right or left as he faces the target.

On firing at the various distances of thirty, forty, fifty, and sixty yards, he will be astonished at the deflection of the shot through the force of the wind; and will find his charge driven considerably to leeward.

By neglecting to make due allowance for deflection when shooting in strong winds, it is impossible to kill at long ranges.

RANGE.

Range is the rock upon which many sportsmen wreck their best chances, the eye being the only guide on which to rely when out in the field; and

the judgment must be formed instantly on a bird rising, as to whether or no it is within range: and when
it is within, the sportsman must be able to measure
with his eye, and that only, the most certain or killing
distance at which to fire.   This may appear difficult;
and, to a young sportsman, it is truly the greatest
stumbling-block he encounters; as he frequently
omits to fire at objects within the best and most
beautiful range, through fancying them out of his
reach; and, on the other hand, he sometimes fires at
objects far beyond the range of his gun.

It will therefore be asked, how is a correct knowledge of the subject to be obtained?- I answer, by
practice at measured distances; and by often measuring, when out in the field, the distance at which he
shot and killed or missed.   This may be done with
very little trouble, and will well repay attention; the
young sportsman has only to provide himself with a
tape, having the distances marked thereon in ink,
from twenty yards up to sixty.   The useful experience he will gain by this simple expedient is great
and invaluable.

Unless a sportsman takes the trouble to measure
distances and try experiments of the kind suggested
it is probable he will remain in ignorance until he

loses his money by a bet with a sporting companion, who convinces him of his error by actual measurement.

Good shots are invariably good and accurate judges of distances; and can measure, with the eye alone, a forty or fifty yards' range with astonishing skill.

Sportsmen will find it much easier to guess distances in small enclosures, and among high hedges and trees, than in large fields and expansive moors. In mountainous districts, sportsmen frequently make mistakes in regard to distances; particularly those who have been accustomed to level country.

In Scotland, too, the mists which are sometimes prevalent on the moors, render it extremely difficult to judge with accuracy as to distances.

THE THREE DEADLY RANGES.

There are three deadly ranges for the gun; viz., point-blank range, short range, and long range.

Point-blank range is that at which you fire without making any allowance in your aim for the motion of the bird or other object, or for gravitation or deflection of the shot.

Point-blank range can seldom be relied on at flying objects, beyond the distance of twenty-five yards.

Short range is beyond point-blank range, but less than long range: it is that distance at which, with judicious aim, an object may be killed with certainty; and may be said to be any distance between twenty-five and forty yards.

It is also sometimes called ordinary range, deadly range, and certain range.

Long range, though one of the three deadly ranges, is a distance beyond that at which a good shot is certain to kill, though his aim be ever so accurate: therefore any distance beyond forty yards is termed long range.

All shots which are doubtful, because of the long distances at which they are fired, though not actually out of range, are at long range. The terms doubtful range, and uncertain range, are sometimes applied instead of the term long range.

With judicious loading, and a regard to the principles of deadly range, a partridge may be killed with certainty at forty yards; but not always with an over or under charge of either powder or shot, because of the uncertain and irregular spread of the shot, when the gun is disproportionately loaded.

The chances are three to one that a good shot will kill at any distance up to fifty yards ; he is certain at forty, if he takes pains to do his work well. With an extraordinary sharp-shooting gun he will kill up to fifty-five or sixty yards, but not always ; though if a perfect master of the art of shooting flying objects, he may kill two out of four at those distances ; but not with an ordinary gun.

Partridges may sometimes be killed at seventy and even eighty yards, but never with certainty : no, not by the best shot in England, with an ordinary gun and loose charge ; because no small gun will throw shot compact enough to make sure of touching a vital part in so small an object, at those distances. Forty to fifty yards are the very outside at which certainty exists. A " dead shot," or any one who fires at birds beyond those distances, cannot be certain of killing. One or two grains of shot would probably be all that struck the bird ; and that is not sufficient to bring it down, unless hit in a vital part, or a wing-bone be broken. A bird possesses few parts that are actually vital ; and a partridge or grouse is ·a small object when its feathers are plucked off. Sportsmen who fire at long ranges should not forget these facts.

It is wanton and cruel mischief to shoot at unreasonable distances, with no possibility of killing: besides too, it disturbs the game uselessly, to say nothing of wounding it in an unsportsmanlike manner.

STRAIGHT-FORWARD SHOTS.

"But when the bird flies from you in a line,
With little care, I may pronounce her thine."
MARKLAND.

These are the easiest of all flying shots; and those which the young sportsman first succeeds in. At a bird flying straight away from the sportsman, his aim should be the top of the back of the bird, if within twenty or thirty yards; and just above the back, if beyond that distance.

From forty to fifty yards is the extreme distance at which a partridge or grouse can be killed when flying rapidly in direct line from the shooter.

They may be wounded in the rump at a farther distance, but are not likely to be hit in a vital part: consequently, though wounded, they do not fall dead.

CROSS SHOTS.

When a bird crosses to right or left of the sportsman, within thirty yards, his aim should be at the head, if flying steadily; but if flying swiftly, an inch or more in advance of the head; if forty yards, five, six, or eight inches; and so, more or less in advance according to rate of flight and distance.

If a bird crosses very swiftly at right angles, sixty or seventy yards from you, in order to kill it you must not only aim one, two, or three feet in advance of its head, but also two or three inches above it.

If the bird crosses to the right, throw your head over the gun, and shoot well in advance.

Among cross shots may be included rectilineal, oblique, acute, and obtuse angular flights; also transverse and curved lines of flight, with some others; all of which require a due allowance according to velocity, and the acute or obtuse nature of the angle or lineal direction of the flying object.

Never refuse a cross shot, though it be fifty or even sixty yards off. Cross shots may be killed at much greater distances than straight-away ones, for two reasons: one, because the more vulnerable part of the bird or animal is exposed to the fire; and the other, because the shot strikes with much greater force at a crossing object, than at one flying in the same direction as the shot.

When a bird crosses to the left, step forward with the right foot; and *vice versa* if it crosses to the right. The reason for this suggestion is very clear: if the right foot be first when the bird is crossing to the right, it is very difficult to bring the gun round far enough without turning the body; and the necessary turn may be instantly dispensed with, by bringing the left foot forward.

When a bird rises very close, be in no hurry to level the gun: it is the protracted levelling that often causes young sportsmen to miss; the hand becomes unsteady through it, and the eye is less to be depended on.

DESCENDING SHOTS.

When a bird is flushed on a hill, its flight is almost certain to be in a descending direction; the aim in such case must therefore be both low and in advance of the bird, when crossing to right or left; and when the direction of its flight is in a straight line, descending from the sportsman, the aim should be at the legs of the bird, if within thirty or forty yards; and below the legs if beyond that distance.

The young sportsman should also bear in mind, that when a bird approaches a high hedge it rises in flight; and immediately on clearing the fence it descends.

These minutiæ, though seemingly of trifling importance, are highly essential considerations for the aspirant to good shooting; and should never be lost sight of in the field.

PERPENDICULAR SHOTS.

"When a bird comes directly in your face,
  Contain your fire awhile, and let her pass,
  Unless some trees behind you change the case;
  If so, a little space above her head
  Advance the muzzle, and you strike her dead."

MARKLAND.

Many sportsmen, who in all other respects are good shots, almost invariably miss a bird flying directly overhead, particularly if it be in rapid flight, or going down-wind.

A great deal must depend on the altitude at which the bird is flying; but in general, these shots are

missed through firing too soon, or too late : the one
as the bird approaches, the other after it passed
overhead. If sportsman could only consider and
practice a few perpendicular shots, they would find
none are easier : there is plenty of time for deliberation when the bird is seen approaching. The instant
it comes nearly over your head, lean back, take a
good aim, and fire several inches in front, according
to the speed or rate of its flight, and you are certain
to kill : whereas, by firing at the breast as the bird
approaches, if your shot strike, they probably glide
off the feathers without penetration through the skin :
and by waiting until the bird has passed, you lose
your very best chance ; because, independently of
the greater accuracy of aim, you lose the additional
effect produced by the bird being at an acute angle
with the shot. By shooting perpendicularly, you
have also the chance of a second shot in the event of
missing the first.

One caution is necessary in regard to perpendicular
shots : the gun should be placed to the shoulder as if
for a horizontal shot, and the sportsman should lean
well back. If the heel of the gun be erroneously placed
on the top of the shoulder, and so fired perpendicularly, it will inevitably break the collar-bone. The

author of "The Wild-Fowler" warns his readers as to this danger, in the following words: "A small gun, loaded with only two drachms of powder, will break a man's collar-bone if fired straight up in the air from his shoulder—the man standing upon hard ground. Accidents of this kind frequently occur at rook-shooting parties, through firing from positions directly beneath the birds."

WIPING THE EYE.

This is a common term among sportsmen: with the vulgar it is erroneously termed "wiping the nose." It occurs in this way: when two or more sportsmen are shooting in company, and one of them fires at a bird and misses it, another fires at the same bird and kills it: it is then said, to the honor of the one who killed the bird, that he "wiped the eye" of his companion who shot at and missed it.

FINISHING LESSONS.

A sportsman who is ambitious to become a dead shot, must not be content with simply winging or wounding his birds at forty yards, or other fair distances; he ought to kill, so that the bird lies at the spot where it fell, and may be recovered 'after reloading, without the assistance of dogs. To wing or wound is only excusable at long range, or random, doubtful, cramped, or difficult shots.

A dead shot kills his birds in the air; they drop dead to his unerring aim, and yet they are not mangled or disfigured. Such men are naturally good judges of distance, accurate marksmen, and instant or simultaneous trigger-touchers; and thus they kill their game in splendid style.

A professed good shot ought always to kill a brace out of every covey that rises before him within thirty-five yards.

Confidence, perfect self-composure, a quick eye,

steady aim, and good judgment, are all essential qualities in a good marksman; and the hand and eye must act in unison; or as if connected by electricity.

No sportsman can shoot well, though with the best gun ever made, if he be nervous, hesitating, flurried, hasty, or careless. The error, more frequently than otherwise, rests in the hand which touches the trigger, being too late in obeying the eye and the aim.

The slightest tremor, one nervous motion, one pulsation of the heart at the instant of pulling trigger, and the steadiness of the aim is lost, and consequently the bird is missed.

So faithfully must the bird be covered at the moment of taking aim, that, when flying across or transversely, in order to kill it, whilst you are pulling trigger you must sometimes absolutely lose sight of it, by reason of the bearing of your gun being both above and in advance of it.

Great attention and steadiness are required in *presenting* the gun at a flying object, it is of as much importance as taking aim. Pitch the gun into its exact position at the shoulder, and the instant you feel that your eye is right, if the trigger-finger obeys, you may be certain of killing.

To avoid missing a cross-flying or running object,

you must not only aim before it, but take care that you do not involuntarily stop the motion of your arms and gun, as they follow the object at the moment of pressing the trigger. Want of attention to this simple fact is too often the reason why the shot passes below and behind the object. Accustom yourself to keep the gun to the shoulder after you have pulled the trigger, and you will eventually overcome this great defect in your shooting, and thereby gain a capital point towards becoming a dead shot. The contrary habit, when once acquired, is very difficult to correct, and often prevents a quick, sharp-sighted sportsman from ever shooting well.

When the bird is flying rapidly to right or left, let the motion of the gun be kept up whilst, and for the instant after, pulling trigger: the space of a yard in flight is gained in a moment.

It is the interlapse between the correct aim and the touch of the trigger, or impulse of the shot, which is the secret of many a miss at a rapidly flying object.

If you find from repeated experiments that you shoot too low, make a firm resolution, and constantly bear it in mind throughout the day, to shoot higher.

Mr. Blaine, in his "Rural Sports," says, "Shoot at

the head in every direction, if possible;" adding, that
he "cannot see any necessity for greater allowance."
But such theory can only be applied to objects within point-blank and short ranges; because experience
teaches us that considerable allowance *must* be made
for distance and velocity of flight.

When a snap shot offers, fix your eyes immediately
upon the object; and, if a bird, pitch your gun well
forward, and fire without an instant's deliberation.
If at a rabbit whilst darting into cover, fire in advance
of its head. It is of no use shooting the hind-quar-
ters of either rabbit or hare, nor the legs and rumps
of birds; because, although you may wound, not one
in ten is recovered; they get away and die a lingering death.

The man who would shoot flying objects with skill
and precision, requires a combination of steadiness
and dexterity in his movements; and there must be
a sympathetic action between the eye and hand.

Many ardent sportsmen never become good shots,
though in constant practice, through a want of these
qualities.

Remember, also, that it is the dumb sportsman
who gets nearest to his game, not the talkative one.

Follow up a trustworthy dog, even to unlikely

5

looking places. He who follows his dog up closest, makes the heaviest bag.

The art of measuring distances with the eye is a great accomplishment in a sportsman, and is of essential value; it is to be acquired by practice, and by shooting at a mark from various measured distances within reasonable range.

A dead shot is enabled, from practice, instantly to calculate the speed, distance, and direction of flight of the object of his aim; if it were not so, he could never be certain of his bird.

And the simple fact that there is a tendency towards the earth in every inanimate substance moving by force through the air, is too frequently lost sight of; whereas no sportsman can ever become a good shot, or kill objects at long distances, unless he has a tolerably correct knowledge of that indisputable law of nature.

Never let a fair chance slip away; that is to say, if a bird rises within range, down with it. Though it rise ever so suddenly, and the surprise be ever so great, if your nerves are quiet and your aim true and steady, the bird is yours.

THREE GOLDEN SECRETS.

There are three elements in accurate shooting at flying objects which, though before mentioned in detail, I would fain repeat for the purpose of impressing them upon the mind of the young sportsman as "golden secrets." They are these:

1. At straightforward shots keep your head erect, and let your line of aim (or visual line) run along the back of the bird at the instant of pressing the trigger; and you may then be certain of killing.

2. At a bird crossing to the right, throw your head well over the gun, and let your visual line run level with the head of the bird, and more or less in advance, according to distance and the rate at which it may be flying when you shoot.

3. At a bird crossing to the left, keep your head straight, pitch your visual line upon a level with the head of the bird and in front of it, at a distance varying from one to twenty-four inches or more, according to range and velocity of flight.

Without a strict adherence to these three rules it is impossible for any man to become a dead shot; whereas by following them up to the very letter, a

bad shot will assuredly become a splendid marksman.

THE MAN WHO NEVER MISSES.

The young sportsman should never vex himself by
reckoning the number of shots he has missed. It is
well to think nothing about them; because missing a
number of shots, whether successively or otherwise,
when out in the field, is no true test that the sportsman is a bad shot.

The most faithful test is, the result of the whole
day's shooting; or the average of several successive
days.

We often hear romantic tales of great performances by sportsmen; some of whom are said " never
to miss :" others, that " so sure as the cap explodes,
the bird falls;" all which may be true in theory, but
not in practice. I have frequently been out shooting
with those who bear these enviable characters, and
with some who are acknowledged to be the best
shots in England; but I never yet saw the man who
could sustain the character, during two successive
days, of " never missing," provided he fired every
time he had a chance of killing.

A good shot may go out in September, and shoot
from morning to evening without missing; or he
may bag as many birds as he has made shots; but to
do this he must fire only at point blank and short
range, and refuse all *doubtful, difficult,* and *cramped*
shots; for it stands to reason that he cannot be certain of killing any of these three at long range;
though chance and good skill may enable him to kill
half the number, or two out of the three; but it is
absurd to imagine he can kill all. One doubtful, difficult, or cramped shot at long range, when successful,
is, to an old sportsman, worth half-a-dozen easy or
certain ones : he delights in it because it was doubtful; and he knows besides, that it taxed his skill to
the utmost ; and no good shot, or aspiring sportsman,
will care for missing any but downright fair and easy
chances.

Therefore when I hear a man boasting of having
been shooting all day, and filled his game bag " without missing a single shot," I am always well convinced that he must have made all the very favorable
shots, and refused many, if not all, the doubtful and
difficult ones; whereas those are the very shots at
which he should have tried his hand.

To constitute a " dead shot" it does not follow

that he should kill every time he presses trigger;
because if he makes random shots it is impossible
but he must sometimes miss, or at least that he cannot always kill; though he may always either *wound*
or kill.

Let me console the young sportsman with the
fact, that the most skilful, the most experienced, and
the deadliest shots, *sometimes* miss fair chances;
though, certainly, very seldom.

Very long shots are always chance shots; and to
one successful there belongs three unsuccessful. For
notwithstanding that the sportsman's aim may be
correct, the scattered and uncertain hitting of the
shot, makes it three to one against killing a very long
shot; or any thing over fifty yards. The proof of
this statement is exceedingly simple: let the sportsman measure the distance, put up a quire of large
sheets of paper, and fire at it; and he will be surprised to find how widely scattered the shot strikes
at long distances; and how easy it is for a bird to
escape, though the aim taken be as accurate as possible.

THE BAD SHOT.

A bad shot is an unfortunate being; generally an excitable, nervous, craving sort of a fellow, who vexes himself every time he fires his gun: and though his companions ridicule his attempts, they are annoyed to see him banging heavy charges at coveys, wounding several but killing none. His dog becomes suspicious of him, and grows careless in its work; because it so seldom has the chance of mouthing, and sticking its nose into the plumage of a bird; which is always as great a delight and satisfaction to a dog in the field, as are the choicest and most fragrant exotics to a lady in her boudoir.

If the bad shot by any chance happens to bring down a bird, a race immediately ensues between him and his dog, as to which will be first to recover it.

Being no judge of distance, he fires either too soon or too late. If he kills, in the one case the bird is so mangled that it is not worth the cooking; and in the other, it is only winged, or so slightly wounded that it occasions more trouble in the retrieving than it is worth. Well may the poet say of him :—

" There sprung a single partridge! hah! she's gone!
Oh! sir! you'd time enough, you shot too soon;
Scarce twenty yards in open sight! for shame!
Y'had shatter'd her to pieces with right aim!"

When he has been over a manor abounding with
birds, and returns home with a brace or two only, he
feels bound to acknowledge the fact of there being
plenty of birds, but says " they are wonderfully
wild."

When shooting with other sportsmen, he invents
all sorts of false excuses to account to them for his
bad shooting: says it is a most unusual thing for
him to miss two successive shots: and then, on missing a third, appeals to his companions as to whether
or no they saw the feathers fly: and on their laugh-
ing, or replying in the negative, he says—" Bless me!
why I completely flecked it!" " Legs are broken!"
" Bird will die!" " A little too far!" " My shot is
too small!" and such like excuses, which continue
throughout the day, and increase the merriment of
the sportsmen, at the expense of the bad shot.

He is, besides, self-conceited, and says the art
of shooting may be better learned without a book,
and so he never reads one.

His friend, a dead shot, tells him that many a bad

shot has been made a good one through the study of
a good book upon the subject. He does not believe
it; therefore his friend the dead shot leaves him, and
says to himself, as he shoulders his gun—

"Where ignorance is bliss, 'tis folly to be wise."

I know one or two affected sportsmen who, rather
than have it thought by their friends that they are
bad shots, actually purchase game and send it as
presents, when they are unable to shoot any.

All bad shots shoot both behind and below their
birds; consequently whenever they chance to knock
a bird down, it is never hit in the head, but almost
invariably in the legs and rump—the least vulnerable
parts; and so there is always a difficulty in recovering it.

Again, bad marksmen seldom kill cross shots, because they shoot *at* their birds instead of *in front* of
them.

As a general rule, a bad marksman kills nothing
but straightforward shots; and those only at point-
blank or short range.

Let me remind the bad shot, that unless he occasionally kills a few birds, his dog will attempt to
kill some for him; and, in bitter disappointment at

5*

his master's fruitless attempts, will run in, chase, and perform many other uncontrollable actions.

A young sportsman should beware of purchasing a dog, however cheap in price, and however well-bred, of a man who has the notoriety of being a "bad shot."

THE NERVOUS SPORTSMAN.

There are many sportsmen who, do what they will, cannot avoid a painful trepidation, palpitation, or state of nervousness when walking up to the dog at its point; and the same if a bird or covey rises suddenly, without being pointed by the dog. Such feelings and pulsations are, of all things, the greatest drawback to good shooting. Many say, "Oh! if I could only throw off this nervous anxiety, this eager desire to kill, this fluttering of the heart when a bird rises before me,—if I could but take these things coolly, and treat them as of less importance, what an excellent shot I should be!"

An ungovernable nervousness is a great and almost insurmountable obstacle to a man ever becoming a proficient in shooting. If such a man ever shoots well during the day, it will be at a moment of unconcernedness, or when he is quite indifferent as to the result.

The only remedy that can be suggested is, to endeavor to recollect yourself, make coolness a duty, and be less anxious and eager as to the result of your shot.

If a young sportsman who is troubled with the "nervous anxiety" were to say to himself before firing, "Steady, Ed'ard Cuttle! steady!" and act up to it, ten to one but he would soon find himself considerably improved.

But coolness and deliberation are difficult qualifications to teach, whether verbally or by book; they should both be inherent in the sportsman, or he must never hope or expect to become "a dead shot" at all times; though when perfectly free from tremor or excitement, he may shoot as well as the best shot in the land. Such a man, however, will seldom shoot two days alike.

Over-eagerness often begets nervousness and confusion, which not only incur danger, but assuredly prevent a young sportsman from killing at the most reasonable distances.

A steady hand, and firm, but quiet nerve, are among the highest and most necessary qualifications of a good shot.   If possessed by the sportsman, he is certain, with perseverance and practice, to become a dead shot.

Successful shooting, gives ease to the nerves and confidence to the shooter; but the fear of not hitting, and the over-anxiety to kill, are the certain precursors to missing.

Nervous men generally find the greatest difficulty in keeping themselves from excitement when a bird is coming directly towards them, or when they are certain of a shot.

When a man is tremulous or excited, whether at the noise or suddenness of birds springing from the ground, or otherwise, he makes an unsteady and different aim to that which he would take if free from tremor and excitement.

Nervous men generally shoot best when by themselves.   In presence of strangers they invariably shoot badly ; some through the vexation and annoyance of being considered bad shots, of losing their reputation, or of being beaten by inferior sportsmen.

Most men shoot well or ill, according to the state of their nerves.   One of the best shots I ever saw in the field, I one day met at a pigeon-shooting match ; when, not being accustomed to pigeon-shooting, to

my astonishment he was in such an anxious and nervous state, that he was well beaten by young sportsmen of very ordinary pretensions.

When the nervous sportsman misses, it is either
because his trigger-finger is not quick enough in
obeying his aim, or because he makes a nervous
twitch at the moment of pulling trigger, and so drops
the muzzle of his gun just sufficient to miss his aim;
or, having got the right aim, he does not keep the
gun moving as the bird moves, long enough to ensure the shot striking where he wishes.

It is impossible to attach too much importance to
these principles; a neglect of them is frequently the
cause of missing a very fair shot; for if the finger
errs in any way, or fails to act in concert with the
eye, the bird is enevitably missed. There must be
no momentary pause: the object is on the move: an
imperceptible instant between the moment of true
aim and pressing the trigger, causes a delay in the
ignition of the powder; and so the bird flies away
unhurt, by reason of the shot flying below or behind it.

THE CARELESS SPORTSMAN.

A blooming youth, who had just passed the boy,
The father's only child and only joy,
As he intent designed the larks his prey.
Himself as sweet and innocent as they,
The fatal powder in the porch of death
Having in vain discharged its flash of breath,
The tender reasoner, curious to know
Whether the piece were really charged or no,
With mouth to mouth applied, began to blow.
A dreadful hiss! for now the silent bane
Had bored a passage thro' the whizzing train,
The shot all rent his skull, and dashed around his brain!
Unguarded swains! oh! still remember this,   .
And to your shoulder close constrain the piece,
For lurking seeds of death unheard may hiss."

MARKLAND.

.

If with no other motive than that of humanity, I should feel perfectly justified in introducing the remarks I am about to make, on the causes and means of prevention of gun accidents; but in addition to a humane motive, it is considered of so much importance to the young sportsman, that he should thoroughly learn and practise the safe and careful mode of handling his gun (and such is the only correct one), that the oldest sportsmen declare it to be the primary lesson he should learn, and one of the most essential rudiments in the instruction of a tyro; lest he should become a " dead shot" to some friend, relative, or companion, and so embitter for ever, with sorrow and pain, the future years of his own life, to say nothing of the lasting grief of those who were nearest and dearest in relationship to his unfortunate victim.

Let the careless sportsman remember, that if his gun should burst and be shattered to atoms, though he may with money get another; yet if his right hand happens to be blown off or shattered, all the money in the world, and all the surgical skill on earth, cannot give him another like the one he has, at a careless and unguarded moment, lost; to his sorrow it is lost for ever.

Therefore, before touching powder and shot, let the young sportsman practise for several days or even weeks, as suggested in the early pages of this work, the safe and proper positions of handling, loading, carrying, and presenting his gun; and after he has learnt these thoroughly, let his tutor fine him every time he catches him off his guard, or with his gun in a dangerous or improper position in his hands. Having well learnt the manipulation, let him practise with gun-caps (upon old nipples) in aiming and snapping them off at objects far and near; and when his tutor thinks him entirely careful with his piece, and fully awake to the dangers of carelessness, then, and not till then, should he be allowed to use gunpowder. And when so far advanced, it becomes necessary that he should learn how to protect himself from danger, and guard against the many accidents to which he himself is exposed, on carelessness, or improper handling and loading the piece.

The young sportsman, having imposed upon himself the strict observance of all the safe modes and positions of handling and carrying the gun, it will, eventually, become more natural to him to carry it in a safe position than in an unsafe one; and then in the event of accidental or unintentional discharge, to his comfort and satisfaction it will do nobody any harm. Through life he must never, under any circumstances, forget, or ever fail to observe most strictly, the lessons he has learnt on the safe handling and carrying his gun.

Any person who has been drinking freely should not touch a gun until sober; and a sportsman should not, under any persuasion, be induced to walk out, or even remain in company with another who is in the least degree the worse for liquor, and yet has a load-

IN IMMEDIATE EXPECTATION OF A SHOT.

ed gun in his hands. The best plan is to take the gun from him unawares, and fire it off.

Strong drink has been the cause of many fatal and lamentable accidents with fire-arms.

Never suffer a gun, whether loaded or unloaded, to be pointed *for a moment* towards any human being. A gun has often been found to be loaded, though the owner has asserted positively that it was not.

Never beat the bushes with your gun, or poke it in a rabbit's burrow.

It is awkward, improper, and dangerous to carry a loaded gun with the muzzle pointed downwards. Such a practise has been the cause of more accidents through barrels bursting than any thing else; a charge of shot is like a small heavy weight in the barrel, pressing upon a movable gun-wadding; and, with the least jar whilst the muzzle is pointing downwards, it is very apt to force its way from the powder, and move the shot-wadding from its position; particularly if the gun be very smooth and clean inside, or if the waddings be thin, or the edges greasy. It is scarcely necessary to add that, as a natural consequence in the event of the shot moving from its position, and so creating a vacuum in the barrel, it will be almost certain to burst on discharge.

Also if you happen to fall whilst carrying the gun in that improper position, and the muzzle should pitch on the ground, and cause the gun to explode, the barrel or barrels exploded will assuredly burst ; and the chances are ten to one but you will be killed.

I once had a narrow escape of an accident of this nature. On stepping out of my gunning-punt in frosty weather, with a loaded double-barrelled shoulder-piece under my arm, and my hands and pockets so full of wild fowl that I fancied I could not carry the gun in any other than that unsafe position, with the muzzle pointing downwards; though I had taken the precaution to put the hammers at half-cock ; I accidently trod upon a piece of ice and slipped, when, having heavy water-boots on, I could not recover myself; and falling forwards, the muzzle of my gun struck into the ground, both barrels plugging up with the sand : fortunately neither barrel exploded, or, as an inevitable result, I should probably have been killed on the spot. On drawing the gun out of the ground, I found the muzzle had penetrated several inches, leaving holes in the sand resembling those made by boring pieces out of a cheese with the tasting knife.

One of the most common causes of guns bursting

is that of accidently stopping the muzzle with clay or snow; through carelessly and improperly carrying the gun with the muzzle downwards, and so climbing hills, hedges, and ditches. A gun may also be instantly burst by firing it off whilst the muzzle is thrust several inches into the water.

Warnings occur every year, of painful and melancholy accidents, many of them embittering the honeyed cup of sport with a gall of bitterness that rankles in the bosom of a reflecting sportsman all the days of his life.

Always take the caps off the nipples before getting into a vehicle, or riding or driving a horse.

Beware of the danger attending the constant practice of drawing the shot from the barrel by inverting the muzzle and tossing it into the hand whilst the caps remain on the nipples; the safer plan is to fire it off, if too careless to remove the caps before drawing the charge.

Never put a cap on the nipples till the performance of loading is completed.

Never carry a gun with the hammers down on unexploded caps.

And remember, that it is in moments of the greatest excitement that accidents generally occur.

It would seem to be almost unnecessary to remind young sportsman of the perils incurred through loading one barrel of a gun whilst the other is loaded and capped, and the lock at full-cock : and yet in the hurry and excitement of sport, this is a common occurrence with careless sportsmen : and of course accidents frequently occur through it, particularly with common locks; and also with good ones, if permitted to become foul, or if besmeared with impure oil.

If one barrel be charged and capped, whilst loading the other be sure to put the lock at half-cock; and if it be a common or doubtful lock, it will be safer to load with the hammer gently resting upon the nipple. The best and safest locks are those which have patent stops for locking the hammer, and holding it in perfect safety during the process of loading.

When the ramrod becomes accidentally set fast in the barrel of the gun, never fire it out; by so doing, you incur great risk of bursting the gun. The foolhardy, in their eagerness and haste, disbelieve these facts, press the trigger, and then the sad truth is verified.

And how frequent are the accidents which every year occur through the fatal effects of loading the wrong barrel, or putting one charge on the top of the other, instead of loading the empty barrel! If this be done, and a thin wadding only lies between the two charges, the gun must inevitably be burst on discharge : and it is two to one but the same result would follow with a thick wadding, if the charges of powder are large. Hundreds of sportsmen make mistakes of the kind, and load the wrong barrel; when, if they are lucky enough to discover it in time to draw the charge, they probably save their lives, or at least a limb.

The remedy for mistakes in loading the wrong barrel is exceedingly simple, if careless sportsmen would only observe it. Always make it an established rule, in charging one barrel whilst the other is loaded, to drop the ramrod into the charged barrel and leave it there on each occasion, whilst putting in the powder and shot.

An additional advantage gained by this suggested process is, that you find whether or know the wadding a-top of the undischarged barrel has moved by the jar occasioned to it in discharge of the other.

Some persons shoot half the day entirely with one barrel, whilst the other is charged : this should not be, because repeated discharges are very apt to loosen the charge of the other barrel : and hence the greater necessity for the precaution suggested, of dropping the ramrod over the charge whilst re-loading the empty barrel.

The reckless folly of drawing a gun through the hedge, muzzle first, is so glaring, that one would suppose none but a maniac would do such a thing, and yet we constantly hear of careless young sportsmen being shot in that way. And it is equally dangerous to drag the gun through the hedge the contrary way, because your friend on the other side incurs equal risk of being shot.

A gun should always be held muzzle upwards on getting over and through hedges ; and where this cannot be done, it should be carefully pushed on in front of the sportsman ; who before and whilst getting through the hedge, should constantly watch the direction in which the muzzle is pointing, and see that it is not towards man or dog.

Another common cause of accidents is, through inattention to the locks of the gun. If they become foul or pull heavier than usual, they should immediately be looked to. The use of common oil instead of pure gunsmith's or watchmaker's oil, has often been the cause of accidents through forming corrosive substances on the part of the scear and tumbler.

Let the careless sportsman beware of loading his gun in too great haste or eagerness; gun accidents are always serious and generally. fatal. Let him remember at all times, and in all situations, in the midst of sport, in disappointment, and in glee, that he holds in his hand a life-taking weapon, which requires the most careful management, attention, and watchfulness in order to prevent accidents to himself, his companions, beaters, and dogs.

THE FLIGHT OF GAME.

Although the flight of game is an element of very instructive consideration for the young sportsman; yet, strange to say, all the multifarious writers on guns and shooting have entirely overlooked the subject; with the exception of one author, who has recently produced one of the best and most complete sporting works that ever issued from the press. I allude to the " Wild-fowler," the author of which has been the first to bring forward, specially, to the notice of sportsmen, the essential consideration of flight, as an important element in the art of good shooting.

The author alluded to discusses the subject, as far

as it relates to wild-fowl, in a very able and interesting manner: proving beyond doubt that he is not only a close observer, but also thoroughly well grounded in the true principles of the art of shooting, and an eminently practical sportsman.

The entire absence of a discussion of the subject in all other works on guns and shooting, shows how extremely superficial must be the knowledge of many of those sporting writers who have professed to exhaust the subject of shooting.

I have no hesitation in saying, that if the young sportsman strictly observes the natural laws of flight, together with those of gravitation and deflection, and can at all times keep himself free from anxiety and nervous trepidation, he will, with practice, in a very short time become a "dead shot." I guarantee that no flying object within range would escape his unerring aim. And I may add further, that the more he studies the flight of the objects of his gun, the better he will shoot.

A bird crossing at right angles from right to left, and *vice versá*, sixty yards from the shooter, is calculated to gain on an average two feet of space in flight, whilst the shot is travelling through the air; or, as it may be stated, between the interval of pressing the trigger and the arrival of the charge, sixty yards distant from the gun.

At fifty yards the space gained would be one-and-a-half feet; at forty yards about one foot; at thirty. about half-a-foot; and so on, proportionally less as the distance decreases. But these calculations apply only to birds crossing at right angles; when other lines of flight are taken, such as rectilinear, oblique, acute, and obtuse angles, the space is less.

The simple fact that at the moment of pressing the trigger, birds are sometimes moving faster from the visual line of aim than at others, by reason of the various lines or directions of their flight, is too often lost sight of; though to be certain of killing, the aim must be more or less in advance of the bird, according to the direction and velocity of its flight; and also in accordance with the distance or range at the time of pressing the trigger.

Let any man consider, and ask himself how he can expect to kill all his shots if he fails to present his gun more or less in advance of the bird, according to the direction and velocity of its flight? If he takes the same aim at all times, regardless of these considerations, it is impossible that he can kill any but chance shots.

6

The young sportsman should watch frequently and narrowly the flight of game: let him reflect as he observes their mode of flight, and the various lines or directions in which they fly; let him do this when he has no gun with him; observing the mode in which they rise from the ground, fly, and alight; the noise they make as they rise or fly, or their silence, as the case may be; all which are fitting subjects for the consideration and instruction of the sportsman who would become a " dead shot."

Undoubtedly the flight of game is an important study for the young sportsman who aspires to perfection in the art of shooting; and though I do not pretend to a perfect knowledge of the subject, still I trust I shall be enabled to record a few facts, the result of close observation, which may be of service to the young sportsman in the course of his tuition for the field.

THE FLIGHT OF PARTRIDGES.

The partridge is one of the most powerful birds on the wing of any that exists among the game species. With wonderful rapidity, consequently wonderful power, it rises perpendicularly from the ground into the air on being suddenly disturbed, particularly when in small fields with high fences. Whatever the height of the fence, if within fifty yards of it, the partridge, on sudden alarm, rises as high or higher than the top, at its first spring from the ground.

As the season advances they rise wilder, higher, swifter, and more suddenly. But in large fields, with low fences, they do not rise so high on being disturbed, unless their flight and alarm is very great.

The steadiest flight of partridges is in the morning before ten o'clock; on first finding them previous to that hour, they rise slowly, steadily, and sometimes sluggishly: the young sportsman should be prepared—it is his best chance.

Their longest and wildest flight is made on being disturbed between the hours of twelve and two in the day: particularly if twice or three times within an hour.

Their swiftest flight, and that at which it is most difficult to kill them, is when fleeing from the fright of having been shot at; and also when flying down wind.

When disturbed on the verge of hills and mountains, they do not rise up so perpendicularly as when flushed on level ground.

With reference to the various allowances of aim, to be made for variety of flight and velocity, regard must always be had to the line or direction in which the bird is flying : for instance, the greatest allowance of all must be made for a bird crossing in a direct line to the right or left. The reader will understand that by greatest allowance I mean, the aim must be more *in advance* of the bird for these than for any others.

Whilst taking these calculations into consideration the young sportsman must remember, that although a bird may be killed, almost with certainty at fifty yards, on crossing at right angles from right to left, and *vice versâ;* yet the bird could not be killed at that distance if flying straight from the sportsman, though more than half the shot should actually strike it : the reason is obvious, in the one case the shot, in its progress, encounters a firm object at a right angle : or, as it may be said, force meets force, as the bird flies into the shot ; in the other case it is a race between the shot and the bird ; and though the shot assuredly overtakes the bird, its force is so materially weakened by reason of both substances moving rapidly in the same direction, that it strikes almost harmlessly, or at all events never goes through the skin.

The flight of game is sometimes considerably increased in velocity by a strong wind, when the bird moves with it : and, on the other hand, the flight is sometimes very much impeded when the bird flies against wind : the sportsman must present accordingly.

The flight of a covey of partridges varies very much, as regards distance, according to the country in which they dwell. In level countries they seldom fly very far on being disturbed : but in hilly countries they sometimes fly unaccountable distances. If once they acquire the habit of taking long flights, they are sure to repeat it on being much disturbed. In some places you may often have a mile or more to walk before reaching them again ; and if game is scarce, sport, in such case, is more a toil than a pleasure.

THE HAUNTS AND HABITS OF PARTRIDGES.

Unless a sportsman knows something of the haunts and habits of the objects of his pursuit, his success is, of necessity, very meagre.

Partridges are hatched in the months of May and June : and dry warm weather is most favorable to the hatching. The heavy morning dews are of great

assistance to them in dry seasons. A wet June is
unfavorable for young partridges : the coveys are
always found to be small after a wet hatching season :
and, on the contrary, the coveys are large and strong
if the season be dry and warm.

In the month of September they frequent wheat
and barley stubbles, from sunrise till about nine or
ten o'clock in the morning ; after which, if a fine day,
they resort to turnip fields, vetches, and sunny banks
and places where they bask. About three or four
o'clock in the afternoon they return to the stubbles,
and remain there till sunset, when they go generally
to the upper grass lands to roost, if any are near at
hand ; if not they go to fallows, clover lays, or barley stubbles.

On wet or foggy days they generally remain all day
long in the stubbles, and driest fields they can find.

As a general rule, they prefer light land rather
than heavy.

As the season advances they become more wary,
and are less regular in their habits. But if there be
moors, grass lands, or marshes in the neighborhood,
they are particularly fond of resorting there at mid-
day, or whenever disturbed in the corn fields.

In November and later, they are so uncertain in

their movements after being disturbed, that the sportsman must rely on his own knowledge of their habits, which always have reference to the locality.

About mid-day, and from that till two o'clock, is generally a doubtful and uncertain time at which to find partridges; they go to the ditches and lowlands to drink about that time, in dry hot weather. At about three o'clock in the afternoon they run about again, particularly if a breeze springs up after a hot day.

In rainy weather, or when their feathers are wet, partridges never lie well.

Furze and fern are, in some districts, favorite covers for partridges, particularly after being often disturbed elsewhere.

Partridges like high hedges, small fields, and green crops.

BEATING FOR GAME.

The term "beating" implies, in sporting phraseology, going in search or pursuit of game with dog and gun; or with either, singly, or with one or more attendants provided with staves (or shillelahs as they say in Ireland) for beating the game out of its hiding-place.

It forms, unquestionably, a very important feature in the young sportsman's training: and until he thoroughly understands it he must not expect to make a heavy bag.

To understand beating for game, the sportsman must know something of the haunts of the objects of his pursuit; and their habits at different times of the day; and where and how to find them after they have been disturbed two or three times in succession.

A quiet, noiseless tread is essential at all times in beating for game in open country; but in thick coverts noise is encouraged.

Talking, whether to your companions, beaters, or dogs, is fatal to all attempts to approach game.

The necessity of observing strict silence, especially in partridge, grouse, wild-fowl, and snipe shooting, cannot be too deeply impressed on the minds of young sportsmen; many of whom, say what you will, insist on constantly directing their dogs by speaking to them; whereas the "dead shot" and "old sportsman" are silent, and direct their dogs entirely by waving the hand, and other such dumb signals.

Always endeavor to find your birds as early as possible on your beat: you have then sport before you at once; and a young sportsman is more likely to kill whilst cool and collected, than when tired and heated.

Beat your ground closely, more especially on the first part of your walk : and always remember that a bird which lies close, is worth a whole covey that is wild.

The young sportsman may be assured that he will find it tends very much to his success to stick to one covey as long as he can ; and never to leave the sport in hand for the idea that better may be found elsewhere. The more he knows of the accustomed haunts of the birds in any particular locality, the better will he be able to arrange his beat.

The oftener a bird is disturbed, the less will be the chance of bagging it, unless accurately marked down; because it becomes more and more alarmed, takes a longer flight than when first put up, and hides in a more improbable spot. An exception to this rule is that of the French partridge, which by being disturbed several times in succession, seems to lose its courage, becomes less capable of evading its pursuers, and finally affords the sportsman an excellent opportunity, by rising close at his feet, very near the spot at which it was marked down.

French partridges have such a propensity for run-

6*

ning, before taking wing, that they become tired after being flushed three or four times.

Young sportsmen make a great omission in not beating fallow fields when in pursuit of partridge-shooting : they simply look over the hedge, and on finding a fallow, they pass it by without so much as running the dogs over it. So indifferent are some sportsmen about fallows, that their dogs become careless in their manner of hunting over them ; and unless pressed, will be likely to leave the birds behind, in some remote corner of the field. Both sportsmen and dogs think them, of all other fields, the most un-likely in which to find game: whereas they are, some-times, of all others the most likely; particularly if late in the season. Fallow fields are favorite places of resort for partridges, they delight to bask there on sunny days: and, by reason of the color of their feathers so closely resembling the ground, they feel themselves safer in such fields than elsewhere,—being entirely invisible to human eye at sixty yards, if they remain motionless : besides too, fallow fields are the quietest resorts they can select : no cattle are grazing there, nor are there any laborers about them as in other fields ; and if the enemy should happen to ap-proach, the fallow field is so exposed and open that

he may be detected at a long distance; and then they
sometimes droop their heads and run along the ridges
unobservedly, from one end of the field to the other.
Generally, however, partridges lie very close in fallows, and afford excellent chances to the sportsman.
Many and many are the partridges which an old sportsman kills in the season on the fallows : whilst the tyro
seldom deigns to try them, beyond walking, with gun
upon his shoulder, from one corner to the other just
to make a short cut of it; and as if morally certain
no sport could be had there; instead of which he
ought to try them as cautiously as the stubbles.

To prove the utility of beating fallows, I may men-
tion a circumstance which occurred when I was very
young. Whilst beating an old fallow, in company
with a veteran sportsman, a "dead shot," a covey of
ten partridges got up at our feet : and as all, or most
of them, rose out of a deep furrow, they were in line
with my friend's aim ; and he killed, unintentionally,
four with his first barrel, and one with his second;
and as I killed a brace with two barrels, we bagged
seven birds out of the covey; three only got away,
and those we marked down and shot within a quarter of an hour afterwards. I am not aware that I
ever, before or since, saw a whole covey of ten birds

bagged in so short a time by two sportsmen. I have many times, unintentionally, killed two birds with each barrel: and on such occasions, whenever I have had a bad shot or a young sportsman walking with me, who, although he fired both barrels, either killed nothing or only one bird, I have remained quiet and allowed him to claim the credit of a brace.

On one occasion, whilst walking with a veteran sportsman, a covey of seven birds rose in front of us; and as three got up out of a furrow, a long distance in front of me, I shot as they rose, and killed all three with my first barrel, and another with my second: my friend killing one with his first and two with his second. Then, turning to the boy who carried the game bag, and looking sternly at him, we inquired if he marked those which flew away? "Yes, sir," said the cute lad, "I marked 'em all down, and so did you: the whole covey lie dead within fifty yards of the 'dorgs!'"

Suffice it to say in regard to fallows, that partridges lie more constantly upon them than many sportsmen would suppose: and late in the season the fallows are the first places to which he should direct his steps. In a rough old fallow they often lie on the ground ·il almost trodden upon.

The manner of beating a fallow is, to cross the ridges right and left, not up and down in the track of the plough. Birds cannot run fast across a rough fallow, and by beating it in the manner suggested, the young sportsman will often find the birds lie close as in a stubble.

Meadow and grass lands are also too frequently passed over by young sportsmen, as if improbable places in which to find game: but as the season advances, they are among the most likely places in which to find partridges at mid-day; by which time they are in the habit of leaving the uplands and resorting to moister and cooler places; they get into meadows near the water, ditches, turnip fields, and other cool retreats.

Partridges lie so closely on well-grown grass lands, that the sportsman should beat them well; and, on finding the birds, he may be assured of a fair chance; and they do not often get up all at once out of grass, but singly. If a covey be dispersed in the morning, and driven into a grass field, they will sometimes lie so close that they will have to be driven up within a few feet of the gun. I have, in company with a friend, killed every bird in a covey in this manner.

When partridges have been much persecuted, they

sometimes pitch in most unaccountable places, such as bye-lanes, orchards, and even public highways. Every sportsman of a few years' experience must often have been surprised at the strange places from which partridges sometimes spring, perhaps just at his feet, and at a moment when he is least expecting to find them. It shows that he should always be upon his guard, for sometimes, when not in the least anticipating sport, he is the more likely to meet with it.

Newly made plantations of young trees, where there is long grass at the bottom, are extremely favorable and likely resorts of partridges; they go in search of seeds and insects, which are generally abundant there; and when the birds have been much persecuted during the morning, they are very fond of hiding in such places.

It is a sound rule in partridge-shooting, that whenever a single bird is marked down with certainty, it should be searched for until found. By firmly adhering to this rule, more birds will be bagged in the end, time will be saved, and the dogs acquire a confidence in their masters' apparently superior knowledge of the whereabouts of game.

When a sportsman has been unsuccessful in finding

birds during the morning, and has traversed a wide extent of country which he knows to harbor several coveys, he cannot do better than "double beat," *i. e.*, try the same ground over again, but more carefully; when, as an almost invariable rule, he finds plenty of sport. Facts of this sort seem, at first sight, difficult to account for, but on reflection and experience they will be found correct.

I have known instances in which an old sportsman has followed a young one over the same beat two hours later in the day, and killed a good bag of game; whilst the young one has killed only a brace; and stated, besides, that he saw "only one covey."

In beating for game the sportsman should always give his dogs the benefit of the wind, if ever so soft an air, by entering upon his beat from a leewardmost quarter, and working each field up wind or by a side wind; either of which are favorable to the dogs and the success of the shooter.

In foggy weather partridges lie close, and do not run about much, they are then apt to be passed over unless the sportsman tries his ground carefully.

In hilly countries, whether in pursuit of partridges, grouse, pheasants, or woodcocks, always beat the hills first, in order to find the game; then mark them down into the nether-lands and go and kill them.

.

PARTRIDGE-SHOOTING.

At the beginning of the season partridge-shooting is simple enough; the birds are young and immature, and have not the strength of wing and power of flight to enable them to offer any other than easy shots to the sportsman; but after they are full grown and full feathered, and have become strong on the wing and wild through the incessant persecution to which they are subject, then the vexation and disappointment of young sportsmen commences; on account of the difficulty they experience in hitting the objects of their aim.   The birds having become wary and suspicious, they will not allow the pointer to approach within thirty yards or more, before they rise up in the air, perpendicularly, with startling suddenness and velocity; and then dart off (rising all the while) with wondrous power of flight, borne on swifter wings, and urged through fear and haste to flee the suspected danger; then it is that the young sportsman's skill is truly tested; shooting then becomes a most interesting art, and not one, nor two, nor even three seasons will suffice to make him a "dead shot," without a careful study of the theory and practice of the art.

Nine o'clock in the morning is plenty soon enough to begin a day's partridge-shooting; and five o'clock in the afternoon is quite late enough to continue it in cool autumn weather; except during the hot days of September, when the sport may sometimes be prolonged till six o'clock.

It breaks the haunts of the birds, and makes them very wild, to shoot at later hours; and it is, besides, the certain means of driving them away to your neighbor.

From three to half-past five, in the early part of the season, is often the best time for filling the game bag; the birds are then very much scattered, and are running about in search of food.

When shot at in early season, partridges always fly to turnips or mangold-wurtzel if near at hand.

As a general rule, the afternoon shooting, from two o'clock to four, is considerably better than that between half-past eleven and two; though from nine to eleven in the morning is a very favorable time; much, however, depends on the state of the weather, the scent, and still more on the sportsman's mode of beating.

After heavy rains have subsided and the turnip tops become dry again, birds lie very close on being driven into a turnip field.

In damp or cloudy weather the scent is always strong and good, but in dry or hot weather it is feeble and bad. Just before and after rain it is invariably strong. In very windy weather it is uncertain. During white frosts it is generally good, but in hard dry frosts, with east wind, the scent is feeble.

Always give a dog the benefit of the wind; that is, hunt him towards the wind, not with it. By this means the dog will be enabled to find more game, and the birds will lie better.

The young sportsman will find that birds lie very much better if he can head them, that is, judiciously place himself in such a position that they lie between himself and the dog. This manoeuvre is not always practicable, but when it is so, and the birds are wild, he will find the advantage of it. But do not attempt to head your game too often, as they may be running: and never do so except with a steady old dog that is " up to the dodge."

It improves the hand, the nerve, the confidence, and consequently the shooting, to use the gun freely : do not pick or spare the shots if you wish to become a " dead shot." Many persons, through fear of being taken for muffs, wait for good chances ; and, as these are always few and far between, where game is scarce, an inferior shot, by banging oftener, and at doubtful chances, beats the better shot, who makes a too careful selection.

It must, however, be borne in mind that there is a difference between using the gun freely, and firing indiscriminately at every head of game that rises, regardless of distances and improbabilities.

If the mind becomes agitated on the sudden appearance of game, the sportsman so affected cannot shoot with certainty.

At an advanced period of the season every bird is watchful as a sentry, and extremely suspicious of the approach of man or dog ; then, to my mind, the sport of partridge-shooting is sport indeed ; and a brace of birds bagged in those days is worth two brace of September birds ; being full grown they are full flavored ; and the sportsman having *presented* all his friends with game, then takes care of himself. I will not say *satisfied* his friends, because to satisfy them all would be impossible,—some of the most craving being like the horseleech, crying "Give! give!" from September to February. I knew one covetous old bachelor with whom, if ever I left any thing less than a leash, he always said, "Ah! yes! very kind of you, sir; but where's the other bird?"

The number of birds bagged by a bad shot, at an advanced period of the season, is always very few; particularly in a country where game is not over abundant. Then is the time when you see the boasted "dead shot" who "never misses," firing away powder and shot without adding to the game bag. The best skill of the best shots is required in partridge-shooting when the season is far advanced, and the birds have become truly wild: for then, both with skill and experience combined, the sportsman often fails to bring home a bag that is satisfactory to himself or his friends.

When birds are very wild, the sportsman must be doubly vigilant, and never off his guard; but always ready to fire within a few moments of their rising from the ground. He should shoot whilst they are rising, and before they are well on the wing. The chances of killing are then very much in the sportsman's favor; because the birds look larger, and are more exposed to the effects of the shot, by reason of their feathers being "all abroad," and the vulnerable parts exposed ; and besides, too, the shot strikes with double force whilst the bird meets it on rising in the air, to what it does when the shot overtakes it flying swiftly away.

When partridges are wild, if you expect to make a double shot, and bag a brace out of the covey, be quick with your first shot. Killing double shots in style, when birds are wild, is one of the most distinguished features of good shooting.

The distinguishing marks and tests by which young partridges may be known from old ones are these: in young birds the bill is brown, and the legs of a dusky yellow : in old birds the bill and legs are of a bluish white, the legs being a shade darker than the bill.

Another test is that of suspending the bird by the lower mandible of its bill, holding it between the finger and thumb; if the mandible bends, it is a young bird; but if the weight of the bird's body fails to bend the mandible, it is an old one. These tests, however, like all others, cannot generally be depended on after the month of November ; because the young ones for the most part have, by that time, attained a precise similarity to the parent birds.

It is indispensably necessary in order to keep up a
stock of game, that the vermin should be destroyed.
Every stoat, weasel, polecat, rat, hedgehog, hawk,
magpie, raven, jay, and other destructive creature,
should be killed whenever seen on the estate ; and
their nests and young searched for and destroyed. It
is, assuredly, one of the principal secrets of keeping
up a stock of game. If a manor be watched ever so
strictly, unless the vermin are kept down, there will be
no stock of game. Consider for a moment, if there
be seven weasels on the manor; and at the most
moderate calculation, if each weasel kills only one
head of game in each week, throughout the year,
that is 365 head of game per annum to the account
weasels alone! and others might be estimated in like
proportion ; to say nothing of the tenfold mischief
during the season of incubation, when partridges and
pheasants are seized by these blood-suckers whilst
sitting on their eggs.

COVEYS OF PARTRIDGES.

Young sportsmen, in their eagerness to fill the
game bag, are too often guilty of the wanton and
erroneous indiscretion of firing into a covey of par-

tridges without aim at any one bird ; feeling certain
of killing two or three at the least, but very often
killing none, though wounding several.   Such an
indiscriminate proceeding I need scarcely say is as
unsportsmanlike and injudicious as it is cruel and
unsatisfactory in its results. It is the central shots of
the charge which are the effective ones; and they
cover only so small a space in their flight, that in the
absence of deliberate aim, the chances are more than
two or three to one against killing any out of a covey
of ten or fifteen, unless they happen to rise " all in a
heap," which is seldom.

And, as young sportsmen generally fire too soon,
forgetting that the shot is more effective at a fair
distance than if either too near or too far ; the fact
that the whole covey often flies away, notwithstanding that both barrels have been fired into it, is easily
to be accounted for.

The sportsman should always endeavor to pick out
the old birds of the covey, particularly in early
season, when they are easily distinguished from the
young ones by their larger size, and by their being
the first to rise. The young birds of the covey do
not so soon become wild and cunning, if deprived of
their leaders.

On a covey of partridges rising in front of the shooter, he should not fire at the nearest of the covey with his first barrel, but rather select, as the object of his aim, the farthest or leading bird; he will then have plenty of time to choose his second shot. The sportsman shows good judgment in reserving a near bird for his second barrel.

It is discreditable to a sportsman to shoot more than one bird at a time with each barrel; unless by chance another crosses the one he aims at just at the moment of pulling trigger.

Having selected one of the leading birds of the covey as the object of your aim, keep your eye upon it until it falls to your shot; and though forty others rise in front of you, do not allow your attention to be diverted towards them until you have killed the bird you propose shooting; if you miss it, fire the second barrel at the same bird, lest it should go away wounded.

In course of time (though books may fail to make the impression) the young sportsman will find from experience, that in order to make sure of bagging any at all out of a covey, he must fix his eye steadily and deliberately on one bird at a time; and the instant that one falls to his first barrel, fix the eye on

another, and with the same deliberate steadiness repeated, another falls to his second barrel, and so he
bags a brace *with certainty.*

If a covey be lost in the month of September, the
sportsman may be assured it is not far off, but lies
close, and very probably he has overrun it.

DISPERSED COVEYS.

One of the secrets of success in making up a good
bag in a country where game is scarce, is that of
dispersing a covey; and then carefully marking the
birds down, and flushing them singly.

The manner in which a covey may be dispersed is
this:—when the dog stands, walk round in an extensive circle, and then advance in the face of the
dog, the birds lying between; when they rise, some
will fly in one direction and some in another, and
sometimes almost every bird will take a separate
route. The experiment, however, is not always successful, particularly when the birds are very wild,
though at other times it is easy enough. It should
never be attempted with any but an old or very
steady dog.

Instinct teaches partridges to disperse for their own
7

safety, when they have been shot at two or three times in succession.

If you succeed in dispersing the covey, you will find it necessary to beat for them very closely: dispersed birds lie "like stones on the ground," to use a common phrase; and in general they do not run or move after alighting; but drop, as it were, into a hiding-place; so that the dogs are unable to wind them, except by passing within a few inches of their retreat.

A dispersed covey affords the partridge-shooter the finest sport he can wish for; particularly among tufts of long coarse grass, fern, rushes, or some such cover, into which the birds pitch and squat until fairly kicked out; whilst the dog stands pointing in the most firm and interesting manner, the bird often being within a few inches of the animal's nose.

The mistake of young sportsmen at these, the easiest shots he can possibly hope for, is, that he shoots too soon, and so either misses the bird entirely, or cuts it all to pieces,

> "Spite of the rules of art he must let fly,
> In one of two extremes—too far or else too nigh."

There are certain peculiarities belonging to dispersed

coveys which it is important to the young sportsman to notice. If the covey be dispersed in the month of October, they generally squat several hours in their lurking-place; but they will not lie so long in the month of September; and in wet weather they squat only a very short time, but often commence piping to their mates after having squatted a few minutes.

When dispersed at mid-day, or during very hot weather, they are likely to lie quietly in their places of concealment several hours; particularly if they have chosen the long cool grass of a fen or meadow; it is therefore necessary to search longer and beat much closer than during cool weather.

If the covey is dispersed early in the morning, it will assuredly reassemble within a short time, and the same if dispersed late in the evening.

When closely pursued and often disturbed, they sometimes drop into the most improbable places. Many a good stray shot is unexpectedly made in this manner, at some straggler which has deserted the covey.

TOWERING.

Towering is one of those curious and interesting phenomena which, though singular to behold, is puzzling alike to the sportsman and naturalist. It is more frequently met with in partridge-shooting than in any other sport. Towering is the last gasp or death-struggle of a dying bird when mortally wounded in some peculiar manner; though the precise nature and locality of the wound, which affects the bird so remarkably as to incite it to such an extraordinary and beautiful effort in its dying moments, has never been ascertained with sufficient certainty to satisfy the curious inquirer.

It occurs in this way: the bird after being mortally wounded, flies two or three hundred yards in a horizontal line; and then, by a sudden effort and peculiar flutter of its wings, combined with a strong muscular exertion made in its dying moments, darts up in the air, several yards apparently, in a true perpendicular line, with its neck extended, beak pointing upwards, and wings drooping at its side; when, being dead, it falls as a stone to the ground.

There is no motion of the bird's wings as it rises

perpendicularly; having gained an impetus by the peculiar but desperate flutter before referred to. The position it takes in towering is precisely that of a dead bird when suspended by its beak; with the exception only, that the feet do not hang down, but are drawn up close to the breast.

It has often been the subject of discussion and speculation among sportsmen and naturalists, as to what it is that causes a bird to tower; or rather, in what particular part the bird receives its mortal wound, so as to cause it to perform so pretty an evolution in the air.

Some say it only occurs when the bird receives a shot in the head or brain; others affirm that it arises from a shot going through the liver; others from a wound in the spine; but without asserting any thing positive upon so truly scientific an inquiry, I am disposed to think it arises from a mortal wound in one of the main arteries of the heart. The throat and beak of birds which, in my experience, have fallen dead after towering, I have generally found full of blood.

When birds are struck by a shot in the eyes, and half or wholly blinded, they sometimes hover and twist about in a very grotesque manner; or soar up

high in the air, and then fall to the ground with
wings extended, and not unfrequently head foremost; but that is not towering; a towering bird dies
in the air; it is only in its death-struggle that a bird
actually towers; and when it does so, it assuredly
falls to the ground dead.

I have seen wounded wild-fowl swim round and
round on the water in small circles, as if in great
agony; and on capturing them have found them
blinded in one or both eyes, and bleeding from the
head and eyes, with no other wound about them; a
single shot having struck the bird in the eye and
gone through its head.

I have sometimes seen wounded partridges soar
very high in the air, as if in imitation of the act of
towering, and then fall to the ground, but not head
foremost; nor have they risen up in the air in that
true perpendicular line which the towering bird
takes, nor have they always fallen lifeless : on the
contrary, I have occasionally seen such birds get up
again and fly away. But this is not towering. The
true towering of a dying bird is a very interesting
sight, and no one who has ever seen it would mistake
it for the mock tower of a wounded bird.

Whenever a bird towers, in the strict sense of the

word, it falls to the ground dead; and the sportsman may generally find it lying on its back.

Towering birds are sometimes very difficult to find; particularly if they fly across a field or two before towering, which is very often the case. And there being no scent to help the dogs, except at the exact spot where the bird falls, the retrieving a towered bird depends entirely on the accurate marking of the sportsman or his attendants.

As a reliable and invariable rule, a towered bird never falls so far off as it appears to do to the human eye.

FRENCH PARTRIDGES.

Very little has ever been written on the subject of shooting the red-legged or French partridge. The reason is, probably, that but few of the authors of books on shooting have ever met with them. Indeed, most of our counties are entirely free of the nuisance of French partridges, though I am sorry to say they are nearly as numerous in some parts of Essex, Norfolk, and Suffolk, as English partridges.

It appears that French partridges were first introduced to this country by the late Earl of Rochford, who lived at St. Osyth Priory, in Essex; and the Marquis of Hertford, who had estates in Suffolk; both of whom imported hundreds of eggs, as well as large numbers of the birds, which were distributed over their estates; and in course of a few years they became very numerous. The late Duke of Northumberland also hatched and preserved them on his estates.

The favorite localities of French partridges are hills and fallows; and in winter they often take refuge in woods and thick-set hedges, particularly when closely pursued, or when the snow lies thickly upon the ground.

In the west of England there are none, or at least they are among the *rara avis* tribe. It is probable that this may not be the case many years longer, as they are decidedly increasing in numbers; and are gradually creeping into neighboring counties. Those who wish to be rid of them should destroy their nests in spring, and kill the old birds during deep snows; when they are unable to run, but hide in the hedge rows and neighboring woods.

A wet egging season is even more unfavorable to the hatching of French partridges than of English ones. The French birds will not sit long on their eggs in wet weather, if exposed to the rain; they appear to lack the courage or endurance of English birds; and so forsake their eggs, and take shelter in the hedges. I found many nests of forsaken eggs of French partridges last season (September and October, 1860), in the eastern counties, some of them in an advanced state of incubation.

At the present day, French partridges are looked upon by almost every sportsman as a nuisance; and the flavor of their flesh as inferior to that of the English partridge. They never lie well in the fields; but baffle both the cunning of the dogs and the skill of the sportsman, especially any one unaccustomed to their habits.

If on entering a field the dog stands at a covey of French partridges, the sportsman may be assured they will run some distance before getting up, probably across the field, and then rise a long way out of range; and so they spoil the dog, make him unsteady, over-anxious, and doubtful, with English birds, which would otherwise lie well; but the dog, fancying they are going to run, like French birds, across the field, in his attempts to follow them, puts them up before the sportsman approaches. French birds are always reluctant to fly until they have run

7*

a long distance, sometimes across two or three fields ;
and it is only by a thorough knowledge of their
habits, and by cunning and perseverance, that a
sportsman can get a shot at them. Often when you
think they have all left the field, they get up one at a
time near the fence, close by you, behind you, and
everywhere but where you expect to see them;
rising as noiselessly as possible, and very different to
English partridges, which generally give a startling
warning when they get up, such as may be heard
across the whole field or further.

When much persecuted, French partridges soon
give in; probably they run so much when pursued,
that they tire themselves; and so a bold start often
ends in a cowardly resignation by the bird hiding in
a ditch.

HOW TO SHOOT FRENCH PARTRIDGES.

Having given a brief history of the nature and
habits of French partridges, I will now proceed to
instruct the young sportsman as to the best mode of
shooting them.

In the early part of the shooting season the young
French birds may be killed with the same facility as

English partridges; but, on arriving at maturity, they inherit all the cunning of the old birds; and unless they can be driven into clover-seed, thick stubble, or some such cover, where they cannot run far, they are difficult to get at. In mangold wurtzel and turnips, they will run across the field, in the furrows, just as quickly as if it were a barren plain.

The best plan is, as the season advances, for two or more sportsmen to go together in pursuit of French partridges; and enter the field at the same time, but in opposite directions, one at each end, and both walking towards the centre of the field; this plan generally succeeds, because the birds, by running from one sportsman encounter the other; and very often both obtain good shots, and thoroughly disperse the covey. The scheme answers best on marking a covey into a field of turnips or beet-root, or any good ground cover.

But young sportsmen must be cautious not to shoot each other, nor to fire in any direction towards his companion, who may be approaching from an opposite direction; and never attempt this manœuvre in a hilly field, nor on any but open ground, where each sportsman can see the other all the while.

There is one branch of the sport of French par-

tridge-shooting which affords splendid practice, and
that is, when the snow lies thickly on the ground in
new-fallen flakes. At such a time the birds are entirely at the mercy of the sportsman; they cannot
run far in the snow, consequently are deprived of the
very means of using their cunning, and they hide in
the fences, where they may be easily traced, turned
out, and shot.

The proper way is for two sportsmen to walk
quietly, one on each side the fence, with a couple of
dogs and beaters; the birds are then put up directly
in front of the sportsmen; each of whom confines his
shooting to his own side of the fence. French partridges may be driven out in this manner, and killed
with certainty, by the most ordinary shot.

An experienced sportsman will sometimes kill as
many in a good deep snow, as on the first day of the
shooting season; and many prefer the winter sport
to the best day in the whole month of September : it
is, truly, fine practice where the birds are numerous;
and no matter how wild they have previously been,
the snow so completely tames and deprives them of
the use of their legs, that they fall easy victims. Try
nothing but the fences and small copses; and take
care to mark those down which fly away.

The sportsman always rejoices at the victory which a heavy fall of snow enables him to make over these troublesome birds.

He should take care to be out on an expedition of this kind as early in the morning as possible; and the birds are sure to be found in the fences. If he is desirous of exterminating the race of French partridges on his estate, a week's continuance of deep snows will afford him every opportunity of so doing: the previously wild and unapproachable species can be advanced upon as they skulk in the fences, and driven out at the sportsman's feet; they are thus entirely at his mercy, if he be only a tolerable shot: they are deprived of the very secret of their cunning and means of evasion, which lies entirely in their legs.

The sportsman should spare his English birds in deep snows, if he wishes to preserve them; and keep down the race of the French.

LAND-RAILS.

THESE birds are more abundant in some counties, and in some seasons, than in others: they are delicious eating, though but little larger than a snipe.

Generally speaking they are very easy shots; they

fly so beautifully slow and steady that no sportsman
ought ever to miss a fair chance. They lie remarkably well, and sometimes rise close at the nose of the
dog; at other times they run some distance before
getting up.

Take time, and be steady in presenting, and the
bird is yours.

On being fired at and missed, it is very difficult to
get them up a second time; they run and hide in long
grass, ditches, or whatever cover may be at hand.
They frequently submit to be caught alive by the
dog, rather than risk a second flight within a short
time.

Though a land-rail is remarkably fine eating when
nicely dressed, sportsmen who are familiar with their
habits seldom trouble themselves to follow them
with the intention of putting them up a second time,
particularly if other game is at hand. Unless the bird
is killed when first flushed, he prefers leaving it till
another day, rather than run the risk of wasting half
an hour or more in endeavoring to turn it out of a
thick-set fence or ditch.

GROUSE-SHOOTING.

This sport, as every one knows, commences in England and Scotland on the 12th of August, and in Ireland on the 20th of August; it ends on the 10th of December.

Grouse-shooting is one of the most attractive recreations with dog and gun : at the same time it is an exceedingly laborious one on any other than well-stocked moors ; and, happily for those who possess them, there are many moors in Scotland with which I am familiar, where grouse are as abundant in August as partridges are in September, on the most strictly preserved manors in any county in England. There, are, however, I regret to say, many thousand acres of heather in Scotland, where the familiar note of the grouse is seldom heard, and where the weary sportsman toils hard for sport, but alas ! the moor is barren of the attractive objects of his search. The poachers have so many devices for taking them, and cheap guns have been so freely circulated among the people, that where there are no vigilant gamekeepers, the poachers take the cream of the sport, and skim the moors before the English sportsman arrives.

Grouse require quite as careful watching as pheasants and partridges, or the sportsman will find himself disappointed with his sport.

They are hatched in April or early in May. If the spring is early and warm, it considerably favors their growth, and they become strong and powerful on the wing by the commencement of the shooting season; but if the spring is wet and cold, the broods are small both in number and size of the birds.

Young grouse may be distinguished from old ones by the test of suspending them between the finger and thumb by the lower mandible, in the same way as that for distinguishing partridges.

In strict sporting phraseology, a "covey" of grouse comprises simply a brood; a "pack" consists of several broods assembled together.

Grouse, when very young, are called "cheepers." At the commencement of the season, whilst the birds are young, they are tame enough for any one; but as the season advances, and they become stronger on the wing, they are not to be shot by any but well practised sportsmen.

Whilst the birds are young, they do not fly far on being disturbed, but keep within reasonable bounds. After having been dispersed, they do not habitually assemble again in the evening, like partridges; but sometimes wait until chance throws them again in the way of their companions; which it generally does at their feeding-grounds, or when they go to drink at mid-day.

It is their nature to "pack" in windy weather, and to disperse in fine weather.

In a flat country, grouse are far more unapproachable than on a moor studded with heathery hillocks. The advantages of the latter are two-fold; as it not only affords an excellent concealment to the sportsman and his dogs, but is also a favorite basking ground and cover for the birds.

The sportsman should contrive to come cautiously and suddenly upon hillocks and places likely to hold grouse, by which means he will often secure fair shots, though the birds be ever so wild; they are fond of sitting about hillocks, knolls, moss bogs, and such like.

Advance upon favorite and likely spots from below: never walk down a hill towards a place where grouse, partridges, or other game are lying.

Grouse prefer the cover of thick, short heather to that which is long.

Dispersed grouse, like dispersed partridges, always

lie well; but there is great difficulty in dispersing a pack of wild grouse.

Whenever you are so fortunate as to disperse a covey, mark them down; and then stick to them so long as you know there is one left.

As the season advances, such is the only way of making up a bag.

Good markers are most essential for grouse-shooting; and they must watch the birds very narrowly; often, before alighting, grouse take a turn to the right or left, as if for the very purpose of deceiving the markers. And though you may lose sight of them in the distance, follow their line of flight with your eye, and on their alighting, they may probably betray themselves by the flapping of their wings; which, at the moment of pitching, are often distinctly seen after the birds have been long lost sight of in their flight over the heather.

On being disturbed in the morning, grouse almost invariably fly to lower ground; therefore the sportsman should beat the surrounding hills first, and save the lowlands till the afternoon or evening, which is always the best time for sport with grouse. They are then more easily found by the dogs, because they are moving about feeding.

A good knowledge of the ground, and the favorite haunts of the birds is a great advantage; as is also a familiarity with their habits; though both these vary according to locality.

The worst time of day for grouse-shooting is between twelve o'clock and two. They are then so uncertain, that you know not where to look for them; and the scent is so very feeble, that the dogs cannot help you much.

It is best not to disturb either grouse or partridges too early in the morning; they lie better and are less wild, if left till about nine o'clock; between which time and four o'clock in the afternoon there is abundant time for a hard day's toil; if not a good day's sport.

In the middle of the day, or between twelve and one, grouse and partridges lie quietly without running about; consequently there is no scent, and they are difficult to find; and if found, spring very suddenly.

When grouse are very wild they will sometimes be found to lie well in the afternoon; and then more shots may be had just before and after sunset, than during the whole day.

During wet weather grouse are always wild; the

moor should never be disturbed whilst the heather is wet.

In the early part of the season the old cock often tries the stale dodge of enticing the sportsman away from the brood, by running off in a contrary direction; sometimes showing his head above the heather; and then running off again several yards before rising; and I have occasionally seen old partridges act the same cunning part, when their broods are young.

Do not talk to your dogs or companions when grouse-shooting, such a proceeding is fatal to sport; the strictest silence must be observed, and the dogs hunted by dumb signals, after the manner suggested for partridge-shooting, and under the head "Dog-breaking."

When grouse soar up in the air on rising, the best time to shoot is just at the instant the bird attains its full height, before darting off. At that moment it is nearly stationary, and the shot strikes with full force; and generally, the bird falls dead.

In windy weather grouse are very difficult birds for a young sportsman to kill; they fly at such a rate that they puzzle the best shots sometimes; especially if the bird is an old cock grouse.

The first hard frost always seems to tame them. If the sportsman is watchful for it, and seizes the opportunity, he may generally meet with good success, though the birds were very wild and unapproachable a few days before.

After they become thoroughly wild, none but a quick and good shot stands any chance of killing them.

Packs of grouse are very wary and difficult of approach. The only chance of getting within range is by "driving;" *i. e.*, by sending your marker round to put them up, whilst you lie concealed in their probable line of flight; when, by suddenly rising up just before they pass over, and shooting well in advance (say from one to three feet, according to the rate at which they may be flying), you may sometimes kill a brace with your two barrels; but, unless you are a very quick and good shot, even this expedient fails, so rapid and powerful is the flight of a pack of wild, persecuted grouse.

Young sportsmen will find it extremely difficult to hit driven grouse; practice and dexterity alone can teach him the art.

Should the instructions under the head "Grouse-shooting" appear to the young sportsman to be short and cursory, we beg to remind him that very much of what has been already stated under various preceding heads, applies with equal force to the subject of grouse-shooting; and should be attentively studied by the tyro.

THE FLIGHT OF GROUSE.

There is much variation in the flight of grouse; sometimes, on being disturbed, they mount in the air like a pheasant, before flying off; at others they steal out of the heather as quietly as possible, and skim along within a few inches of the ground. When they soar they are good marks for the sportsman, but when they skim off slily they require to be taken very quick, or they are soon out of range; their flight is very rapid and strong, and unless the sportsman be watchful he will find they have flown several yards before his eye catches them; and it is those which get up at the longest distance that fly low, those which mount are generally sprung close to the sportsman or his dogs; they get up in greater terror, and so soar in the air several yards perpendicularly. Also, if you come suddenly upon them they mount in the same manner.

They take longer flights than partridges; particularly after being often disturbed, and they generally fly down wind. The sportsman should therefore arrange his beat judiciously, and be cautious how he drives his packs of grouse, or he may have the mortification of seeing them all fly to his neighbor's moor, directly after being disturbed.

BLACK GAME.

The sport of black game shooting is similar, at the commencement of the season, to that of grouse-shooting; except that black game are generally found in moister places, particularly in swampy ground, among short thick rushes; on the brown-colored seeds of which they greedily feed.

The season for shooting them commences on the 20th of August, and ends on the 10th of December.

There is one remarkable peculiarity in the habits of black game, that in the first of the shooting season, when they are young, they lie so close that they almost suffer the sportsman to tread upon them before they take flight; but later in the season they become the wildest game on the moors, and are the most difficult of the species to approach.

The scent from black game is very strong to the nasal organs of the dog. They are easily found, and a wounded one easily tracked or "roaded" by a good dog. The young sportsman should use a steady old dog for the sport; he should walk up to the dog when it stands, with a slow and cautious step; and if a good shot, he may bag a whole brood in the space of a few minutes. The birds lie very close on being first pointed, sometimes directly under the dog's nose, and the old gray hen is as reluctant to fly as her young; but, on being closely pressed, she suddenly rises with startling and tremendous flutter, frightening a young sportsman to such a degree that it puts his nervous system into a great state of tremor; so that although a splendid shot offers, and a large mark, he often misses the old hen. If he can command his nerves and take a steady deliberate shot, aiming at the head of the bird, she is sure to fall. Having killed her, let her lie at present; don't speak a word or stir a step, but load again with all possible dexterity, and another shot will almost immediately follow, as one or two of the brood will rise; down with them, and load again quickly as before; advance step by step, slowly and cautiously, being ready for a shot right and left; and so, one by one, the whole brood will get up at intervals, probably all within range ; but if not, carefully mark those which get away ; they will fly only a short distance, and you will have them presently. In this manner every bird may be killed in the brood ; and indeed such is very often the fate of many broods of black game in the early part of the season.

Old black cocks are considered a nuisance to the moor ; they drive red grouse completely off the ground. Whenever a chance offers at a black cock, the sportsman should take care to kill it ; they are nearly as tame as young ones in the early part of the season, but towards autumn they are very shy and wild. At that time they may sometimes be shot by stalking, as they sit perched on a tree or a commanding knoll. The average weight of a black-cock is not less than four pounds. When beating the covers for black game the sportsman must keep a sharp lookout for they are very cunning ; often stealing away to some remote part of the wood, and then going off as slyly as an old fox. Sometimes they sit very close in the thickest part of the underwood ; and when closely pressed, they rise with a great noise and flutter. But whenever they can, they steal away noiselessly ; and perhaps you only get a glimpse of

8

them when out of range.   Black game require a hard
hit to bring them down, more especially an old cock.

Noisy beaters are by no means desirable when
looking for the black-cock in a wood.   They may
beat the cover as much as they like, but the less noise
the beaters make with their tongues the better.

Covers in which the birch and alder grow are the
more favored resorts of the black-cock.

In the heat of the day black game seek a shelter
from the sun ; they are then frequently found in thick
crops of bracken.

Sometimes they visit stubble and corn fields, where
they feed greedily on the ears of corn ; but they have
sentinels on these occasions, and are always extremely
vigilant and suspicious of their enemies.

THE FLIGHT OF BLACK GAME.

The flight of black game is peculiar ; when seen
on the wing at a distance they very much resemble
wild ducks, both in the form of their bodies and the
motion of their wings.   They fly with heads and
necks stretched out like wild ducks ; maintaining a
steady, wheeling, or determined sort of flight.   And
they are much in the habit of following each other in

the same track; therefore if you chance to obtain a shot at black game as is it flying across country, by standing still and watching a few minutes from the same spot, you may probably obtain other shots; particularly if the birds happen to be fleeing from some moor where they have been disturbed by a neighboring sportsman.

Young black-cocks may be distinguished, when flying, by the white feathers in their tails; but in other respects, the plumage of the young cocks is very similar to that of the old females.

The old cock is easily distinguished by his large size and dark plumage.

THE DUTY OF MARKERS.

The term "marker," in shooting phraseology, implies a person whose duty it is to watch the birds in their flight, and mark the spot at which they alight; by which means the sportsman is enabled to follow them up with a greater certainty of sport.

A marker is generally stationed on a hill, in a tree, or some such commanding position; where he may be of great service in marking the place where the birds fly to, on being flushed by the sportsmen in the valleys. It is also a good plan to place a marker on horse-back, and a very usual one in undulating countries, where it is sometimes necessary for the marker to gallop from one eminence to another during the flight of the covey or pack.

Markers should be able to direct the sporstman by signs of waving the hand or lifting the cap.

It is indispensable that a marker should have good eyes, and the longer sighted he is the better. He should also be provided with a small but powerful telescope; particularly when the birds are in the habit of taking very long flights.

Some men are much more useful and correct as markers than others. Some are able to mark with splendid precision at half a mile distant; others are so careless and indifferent as to be of no use at all.

Markers should also, when necessary, look out to place themselves in such a position as to turn or deviate the flight of a covey which may be going in a contrary direction to that desired. This may be done by waving a handkerchief on a stick, or throwing the hat up in the air.

Markers must carry their attention well forward, especially on losing sight of the covey or pack in the distance : both grouse and partridges always turn up the whites of their wings and flap them just before alighting.

The sportsman should never allow two markers to be together; they are sure to talk, and if there is no game near to be disturbed by their chatter, their attention is taken off the duty imposed on them.

In a hilly country you must generally have márkers.

Where game is abundant, markers are a nuisance.

WOUNDED GAME: HOW TO CAPTURE.

Every sportsman on knocking a bird down is anxious to recover it; but many winged and wounded birds are lost by inexperienced sportsmen through haste, anxiety, over-eagerness, or an imperfect knowledge of the nature and habits of winged and wounded game.

All birds, when deprived of the power of flight, feel themselves at the mercy of their pursuers; and it being a struggle between life and death with them, they make the utmost use of their cunning in order to evade capture, whether pursued by man or dogs.

A winged partridge, on dropping into standing corn, clover, grass, or turnips, cannot easily be recovered without the assistance of a dog that will trail it up entirely by the scent. For this purpose a retriever is of great service to the sportsman.

The habits of wounded birds are very deceptive; inexperienced men would be astonished at the distance run in a few minutes by a winged bird, more especially a French partridge; which, if only pinioned, will sometimes run across two or three large fields.

The sportsman, on firing, should not move from his position until he has carefully marked the precise spot where the bird fell. Accurate marking in high grass, corn, clover, or turnips is most essential; and the sportsman who expects to recover his game will do well to pay due attention to the subject. A bird on falling dead, requires equally careful marking; because of there being no scent to assist the dog in finding it, except at and about the spot where it fell.

Retrievers, pointers, and setters, by training and practice, watch the bird in its flight and fall. A clever dog so trained, after waiting quietly whilst its master recharges the gun, will go straight to the spot where the bird fell, and secure it *instanter*. A dog that is clever at finding wounded game, be it of what breed it may, and whether pure or mongrel, is an invaluable animal to a sportsman.

If you lose a bird, by reason of there being no scent, or your dog having taken the wrong scent, or otherwise; and feeling certain that the bird cannot rise again, you leave the spot and go to it again, quietly, in course of an hour or more; the chances are ten to one but you will find your bird.

On one occasion, the season before last, I lost a land-rail in long grass, after fairly knocking it over, and marking to a foot the spot at which it fell. It was a very sultry day, and probably there was scarcely any scent for the dogs, which, besides, were thirsty at the time; and neither they nor my friend and attendant could find the bird. I went an hour afterwards by myself, and there was the bird within a few inches of the spot I had marked, by driving a small stake in the ground. It was wounded in the body as well as winged; and appeared to have just crawled out of the grass to die after we had left.

Wounded game should always be followed up immediately, and energetically searched for until it is bagged.

Whenever a bird twitches at the moment of being

shot at, the sportsman may be assured it is badly wounded, and he should mark it down and follow it up without delay.

If the legs of the bird shot at hang down immediately after the charge, it is almost a certain sign that the bird is mortally wounded; it should be most narrowly watched and marked down.

Any bird from which the feathers fly, or become disarranged on being shot at, is wounded, though not always mortally; such a bird, however, should be immediately followed up.

The necessity of carefully marking a bird whenever it is struck, cannot be too deeply impressed upon the mind of every sportsman who wishes to recover his bird.

More than one half of the birds which exhibit symptoms of being struck by the shot, fall dead within 200 yards of the spot at which they received their wounds. But young sportsmen, in their over-eagerness to mark the covey or those which fly away uninjured, lose sight of the wounded bird, which might easily and certainly be recovered if marked down; and the consequence is, that the bird either falls dead within two or three fields, or it drops to the ground unable to fly or run; and, being unobserved, there in lingering agony it dies. The dogs are very unlikely to find it, except by the merest chance, because it cannot move to disperse the scent; and so, unless the dog happens to pass within a few inches of the spot, the bird is never recovered.

Winged birds, on the contrary, are marked down at the instant, because they fall at once, on the wing being fractured. It is the bodily wounded birds that are so frequently lost.

Grouse sometimes fly away with their wounds to a great distance; it is not at all unusual to recover a grouse several hundred yards from the place where it was shot.

WOODCOCK-SHOOTING.

All sportsmen take great delight in woodcock-shooting: a peculiar charm appears to belong to the sport; no sound is more pleasing to the ear of a sportsman, when beating a cover, than the words "mark cock!" A successful day's woodcock-shooting is in the highest degree satisfactory; and certain it is, that many sportsmen are far more delighted at killing a woodcock than any other bird of the game species. It is a sport which requires a good deal of practice; for although a woodcock may now and then

be killed with very great ease, they are for the most
part difficult birds to shoot, their flight being so uncertain and varied; often dodging through glades
and among trees as if purposely to confound the
shooter. They are so irregular in their flight, that
on some days they are found to fly slowly and lazily,
and to a short distance only; whilst on other days
they fly straight away to a long distance, and quite
out of marking range.

No one can become skilful in the sport without
much practice, and a good knowledge of the flight
and habit of the woodcock. On some occasions they
may be found and killed as easily as young partridges:
and perhaps the very next day they are artful in their
movements, difficult to find, and more difficult to
mark.

Clumber spaniels are the kind of dogs best adapted
to the pursuit; they should be well trained, so as to
be at all times under the perfect control of their masters and the beaters who accompany them. They
should be active and persevering animals, and thoroughly up to the scent and haunts of woodcocks; for
they are birds which sometimes lie very close, and are
sluggish and difficult to flush, though at others they
are very easily put up.

Woodcocks arrive in this country by the first or second week in October, but in greater numbers towards the latter part of that month. November is the prime month of the season for woodcock shooting.

They are to be found in the covers near the sea in October. But if there happen to be no covers near the spot at which they reach the shore, they keep to the open ground, glad to rest their weary limbs by taking refuge in brushwood, furze, hedges, rushes, heather, or whatever temporary cover may be nearest at hand.

> " When first he comes
> From his long journey o'er th' unfriendly main,
> With weary wing the woodcock throws him down,
> Impatient for repose, on the bare cliffs;
> Thence with short flight the nearest cover seeks,
> Low copse or straggling furze, till the deep woods
> Invite him to take up his fixed abode."

Woodcocks are also frequently shot on the moors in the month of October; but directly the frost comes, it drives them to the woods.

They are birds which like to lie in dry and warm sheltered places; they do not go to springs and wet grounds in the daytime, unless very hungry. They go at night to their moist feeding grounds.

A small double-gun, with short barrels, will be found

the handiest weapon for woodcock or cover shooting. Woodcocks sometimes rise very suddenly; and among trees and brush-wood, *one* chance only is generally all that offers. The sportsman should instantly take advantage of it, and fire on the first opportunity; it may be the only one he will have.

In well-grown woods and plantations, on flushing a cock, the sooner you can knock it down the better; shoot, if possible, before the bird rises so high as the branches of the trees. When this cannot be done, endeavor to make a snap shot through the clearest opening that can be found, or through the twigs of the trees.

In covers which are of not very long or lofty growth, time may generally be given for the bird to rise as high as the tops of the trees; but, as a rule, a cock should never be allowed to go far before you shoot.

It is the nature of woodcocks, on being flushed in a wood, to make for the clearest opening, and then soar as high as the trees; over the tops of which they skim off in a straight line, and generally pitch again in another part of the cover, or make a tortuous flight and drop in, or very near to, the same spot from which they were flushed.

A familiar knowledge of the wood and surrounding locality is of essential service to the sportsman; and the more frequently he beats the wood, and marks the line of flight taken by the woodcocks, the better by far will be his success. There is sometimes so much sameness and regularity in the habits of woodcocks, that they may frequently be found in the very same spots from which they were flushed the day before; therefore, after once or twice observing the line of flight in any particular locality, the sportsman is in possession of very useful knowledge as to the best position and route to take on another day; and has considerable advantage over his fellow-sportsmen when beating large covers for woodcocks.

I have often heard it remarked, that no one ever saw a woodcock entangled in the boughs or bushes on rising; though the alarm be ever so sudden and great, it always takes care to choose a place in the wood for its retreat, where there is a clear opening towards the sky, or a glade through which to pass and gain the open.

Woodcocks are in the habit of running many yards from the spot at which they are marked down: the running is performed on the instant of alighting.

On beating a cover for woodcocks, try the holly

bushes and evergreens; they are, of all places, the most likely ones to hold the objects of your pursuit.

A woodcock is generally considered an easy shot to a sportsman; but notwithstanding, there is no bird which is more frequently missed, particularly when found unexpectedly.

It is true that the remotest chance is taken advantage of in woodcock-shooting, and random and useless shots are often made; being birds of passage, and a great prize also, sportsmen are always eager to bag them.

Woodcocks frequently rise within ten or twelve yards of the sportsman, and often so clumsily as to offer the fairest of shots; but they sometimes as suddenly dodge round a tree, or by some other unexpected move, elude the skill of the best sportsmen.

They are often very indisposed to rise from their favorite haunts, and will sometimes fly round the wood as if in search of a secure retreat, and then cunningly haste back and pitch in the very same spot from whence they were flushed. Manœuvres of this kind are inherent in the woodcock, and when viewed from a commanding position are not only interesting to behold, but likewise very instructive to the sportsman; who, if he condescended to become marker for

his friends on one or two occasions, the knowledge
he would acquire of the habits and flight of woodcocks by that means, would be of lasting service to
him as a sportsman.

Markers are of essential service in woodcock-shooting; they should be placed on the most commanding
hill, or in a tree overlooking the top of the wood. A
man so placed, if he keeps a good look-out, will be
enabled to mark every cock that tops the trees; and
they often pitch in such improbable places as few
would think of beating.

It is also necessary, in large covers, to be provided
with beaters, but they should not be allowed to hurry
the dogs: many a cock is left behind through the
beaters being too hasty and eager; and, on the other
hand, many are left behind which might have been
flushed had not the beaters been neglectful of their
duty, through fatigue or laziness.

When the beaters are numerous and very noisy,
woodcocks, on being flushed, are apt to alight on the
outskirts of the covert; therefore, on beating back
again in the same wood, the outside borders of the
cover should be tried.

On flushing a cock the second time within an hour,
the sportsman should take care to kill it; they are

not so regular in their flight on being twice disturbed within a short time.

A woodcock is a much more cunning bird than many would suppose; and after having been shot at and missed, seems to remember it, and endeavors to puzzle its pursuers as much as possible. After being flushed once, they lie very close on an attempt being made to disturb them a second time; so that active beating is necessary in order to put them up.

The sportsman must watch the flight of a woodcock, and endeavor to follow it with his eye from the first moment of its being sprung; he must look out in the openings, and snap a shot on the first opportunity, or the chance of another may be lost.

In long-continued and severe frosts woodcocks desert their inland retreats, and go to woods and cliffs near the sea, generally preferring those on the south coast; their reason for doing so is, that through the severity of the weather, they can obtain no food except on the sands and marshes, which are not severely affected by the frost, by reason of the influx and reflux of the salt water.

> "The woodcock then
> Forsakes the barren woods, forsakes the meads,
> And southward wings his way, by Nature taught

To seek once more the cliffs that overhang
The murmuring main."

Woodcocks seek the sea-coast also in the month of March, and await in the neighboring woods a favorable wind to assist them in their migration to another climate. They are not so good eating in March, because of the near approach to the breeding season.

Woodcocks always prefer such covers as lie with a sloping surface, and aspect towards the morning and mid-day sun. In some places where this choice of retreat is at hand, they number more than two to one in a wood with a sunny aspect than in that with a cold northern one.

Another of their favorite retreats is a sheltered valley in the midst of a wood, or such other places in the cover as are least affected by frost, and most exposed to the mid-day sun.

A wounded woodcock is easily recovered; it seldom runs from the spot where it falls.

THE FLIGHT OF WOODCOCKS.

In no case is the truth of my oft-repeated assertion, as to the necessity of a familiar knowledge of the

flight of game, more fully verified than in the pursuit
of woodcocks.

The sportsman who is thoroughly familiar with the
flight and habits of the woodcock, will be enabled to
kill more than twice as many in the course of the season as he who takes no pains to inform himself on so
instructive and interesting an element in the art of
shooting.

The rate of speed at which the woodcock flies is
deceptive; varying considerably according to the position from which it is flushed, the season of the year,
time of day, strength of wind, &c. Thus it is sometimes slow and labored, at others, twisting, darting,
and dodging, and often rapid and direct as a hawk.
Sometimes they begin with a heavy, lazy flight, and
then suddenly dart away with surprising swiftness.

They have a much greater power in their wings
than many persons imagine; and when suddenly
alarmed and much frightened, they are as difficult to
shoot as snipes. Distance must be less regarded in
woodcock-shooting than in any other sport; because,
by giving time in the hope of getting a better chance,
you lose the only one which offers.

> " Where woodcocks dodge, there distance knows no laws;
> Necessity admits no room for pause."

A woodcock on being flushed in covert, makes directly for the glades, or for the clearest openings, when it soars as high as the trees, and flies in a straight line over the tops. To a sportsman who may happen to be beneath or within range, these are the fairest shots of all in woodcock-shooting. There is so much steadiness in their flight, when once they have gained a clear space above the trees, that by firing more or less in advance of the bird, according to the rate or rapidity of its flight, you are almost sure to bring it down.

Woodcocks make a regular evening flight from the woods to the meadows, fens, and ditches; they go just at the beginning of twilight, and return to the woods early in the morning.

These morning and evening excursions to and from the wood are made with great regularity; if undisturbed, they fly day by day precisely the same route, and frequently to the same places, both in the wood and the feeding-grounds elsewhere.

The regularity and sameness in the course of the woodcock is very remarkable. They appear as familiar with all direct openings and glades in the woods they frequent, as if they had used them for years. Day after day, and week after week, on being flushed, they fly off by the same route, through the same glades, and over the tops of the same trees. Even in the open, their line of flight does not vary twenty yards. They appear to have certain retreats, and certain roads leading to and from them.

It is therefore obvious that the sportsman who is familiar with these habits of usage, by practice, knows to a few yards the spot at which to look out for a shot, on hearing the signal "Mark cock!" He therefore has considerable advantage over one who is not so informed.

It is very necessary in woodcock-shooting to notice particularly the speed at which the bird is flying, and regulate your aim accordingly: no bird is more deceiving to the eye of the sportsman, because it frequently and suddenly changes the rate of its flight from very slow to very fast; and whilst making its way out of the cover, sometimes dodges and twists its course in the most puzzling manner; but it no sooner tops the trees, or gains the open, than its flight is straight and swift.

Woodcocks do not generally fly far on being first flushed; but on being disturbed a second time within an hour or two, they suspect the enemy and go off further; on a third flush they go further still, and so gradually become wilder. A good shot, however, will generally stop a woodcock at the first time of flushing, or, at all events, at the second.

PHEASANT-SHOOTING.

This sport commences, according to Act of Parliament, on the 1st of October. It is considered by some persons as the most princely recreation with dog and gun of any that can be found in this country: but many other persons—and among them some of the most experienced sportsmen and most splendid shots in the land—consider pheasant-shooting the least like real sport of any of their pursuits. However, there are few sportsmen who do not value a brace of pheasants when they shoot them. They look very beautiful in their plumage—they make a handsome present to a neighbor—they form an aristocratic sort of dish, of which everybody generally partakes when he gets the chance; and, when nicely roasted, they are uncommonly good eating.

It is easy to imagine that the strict and extensive game preserver, who estimates his coverts not by acres but by miles, can pride himself by offering his friends incessant shooting throughout any day in

October; pheasants rising right and left at every advancing step : but then the question is—do sportsmen care for such carnage and banging? Some like it for a change, but there are few who care for many successive days' battue.

In my opinion the true enjoyment of pheasant-shooting consists in going out with one or two friends only, where pheasants are neither very tame nor over-abundant.

But pheasant-shooting in closely preserved covers, during the early part of the month of October, is uncommonly tame sport. As the covers become more and more naked, and as autumn advances, so pheasants become more and more wary; and then the sport becomes exciting, the birds become much wilder, and are not brought to bag so tamely as in early season.

When the branches are all leafless, then the real enjoyment of pheasant-shooting is said to commence.

Early in the morning pheasants may generally be found in hedges near the covers, particularly after a rainy night.

About four o'clock in the afternoon is a very likely hour at which to find pheasants in turnips, carrots, or mangold, near the coverts.

Sometimes (particularly after a long flight) they are difficult birds to put out of a hedgerow or thick cover. They lie so close that dogs may pass on both sides, and yet fail to spring them: and they often perch a few feet above the ground, so as to be out of the way of the dogs' noses.

In beating for pheasants in thick-set hedges or coverts, always give your dogs the benefit of the wind, or it is impossible to find them, particularly cunning old birds.

If disturbed in windy weather, pheasants sometimes fly far away down wind: and unless marked down, the probability is that they may never return. They hate windy weather, and seldom fly against strong gales.

There is no better time at which to find pheasants out of their coverts than during the first hour or two after sunrise; at which time they go to stubbles of wheat and barley which may be near adjacent.

A straggler or two may generally be found during the day, in the hedges enclosing the stubbles in which they feed.

Pheasants venture further from the wood in foggy weather: they are then soon bewildered, and know not which way to return. He who would keep his pheasants at home, will not disturb them in foggy weather.

In pheasant-shooting the young sportsman must remember that it is necessary to shoot specially high when the bird is rising perpendicularly, and well forward when it is flying across.

The afternoon is the best time of day for pheasant-shooting; the cock birds, in particular, do not rise well till that time of day.

About two o'clock in the afternoon is the time pheasants roam about for drink; they get into ditches and shady places in dry weather about that hour.

Well-trained springing spaniels are the best kind of dogs for pheasant-shooting; particularly in thick-set coverts.

When the woods are full of hares and rabbits, dogs are not much used in pheasant-shooting, but beaters only: retrievers, if under perfect obedience, may sometimes be employed with advantage.

A pheasant is by no means a difficult shot; on the contrary, to a person accustomed to their mode of flight they are easily brought down. It is the tremendous flutter and whirr they make on rising, which so discomposes the nerves of excitable or over-anxious sportsmen, and so causes them to miss their aim. The poet Watt gives a capital hint, when he says:—

> "Be but composed, and, I believe,
> Your eye will ne'er your hand deceive."

If ever so well fed, pheasants will stray a little. They leave the woods at dawn of day, and again in the evening just before sunset. Gamekeepers are generally vigilant at those hours, and in the morning, as soon as the sun is up, they beat them back into the woods.

A *nide* of pheasants signifies a brood or hatching, same as a *covey* of partridges.

There is great danger in pheasant-shooting in coverts, unless the sportsmen keep in line, as in a battue, and never shoot except far above the range of human head.

Pheasants require vigilant watching in suspicious neighborhoods. They are always a prize to the poacher; and no bird is so simply, quietly, and easily taken by means of snares and other notorious devices.

9

FLIGHT OF PHEASANTS.

Whether viewed on wing or at perch, the pheasant is one of the most beautifully plumaged and gracefully formed of English birds; a cock makes a most resplendent show with its wings extended on a sunny day.

On being suddenly disturbed, the pheasant rises perpendicularly from the ground with strong wing and tremendous whirring: and then having topped the trees, it glides off rapidly to the outskirts of the wood, if a small one; but early in season it is generally reluctant to leave the wood unless hard pressed.

A stray pheasant on being suddenly driven up, often mounts very high in the air, particularly if an old cock.

Many sportsmen reserve their fire until the bird has risen to its full height, and then shoot at the moment of its darting off over the tops of the trees; but there are many occasions when this delay is unwise, and the shot must be made at the first clear sight.

The startling whirr and flutter a pheasant makes on suddenly rising, when close at the young sportsman's feet, more frequently than otherwise saves its life, by so thoroughly discomposing his nerves that he fires, and, with certainty, misses his aim.

The poet says :—

> "Should pheasant rise, be most particular—
> He rises nearly perpendicular;
> Wait a few seconds till your sight
> Perceives his horizontal flight."

He who would preserve pheasants and keep them to his coverts, must not disturb them too frequently, or numbers will leave the wood never to return.

Pheasants fly further on being much frightened, and stay away from their coverts longer than any other game.

COVERT-SHOOTING,

Or, more properly, shooting in coverts, is a varied sport; some men prefer it to any other. To my mind the most charming branch of it is woodcock-shooting; but as this is already treated of under a separate head, it will be unnecessary to discuss it here. Pheasant and rabbit shooting are also important branches of the sport of covert-shooting; but they also are each discussed under their own heads.

It will, therefore, be only as to the general pursuit of shooting in coverts, that these remarks will be devoted.

Game of all kinds acquire, naturally, the habit of learning in what places they are most secure; and though it is not every species of game which seeks the protection of woods and thickets, there are some species whose home and daily resort is the covert.

As the season advances and the leaves fall, game in the coverts diminishes. The sportsman finds less and less every time he beats the woods. Hares do not like the falling of the leaf; and so many of them leave the wood and get into the open fields; and pheasants shift their ground or move off on the first approach of noise or suspicion.

It is therefore necessary, when pheasants are very wild, to walk through the woods as noiselessly as possible.

When beating the wood for woodcocks or any other game that may be found, it is generally desirable that the beaters should make as much noise as possible, whilst the sportsmen should go on quietly in advance. And the sportsmen who have the good

READY, BUT NOT IN IMMEDIATE EXPECTATION.

luck to walk outside the cover, cannot be too quiet; they should keep in advance of the beaters, but in line with those in the wood.

The gun for shooting in covert should be a short-barrelled breech-loader, about No. twelve gauge, the length of barrels not more than two feet four inches. A gun of this description may be handled and used freely among the bushes, when a longer one would often balk the shooter, through catching against the branches of brushwood.

In beating long narrow strips of copse, the two sportsmen should walk one on each flank, outside the wood; about thirty or forty yards in advance of the beaters, all of whom, with the dogs, should go inside.

Beaters must stop immediately on discharge of a gun, and go on again at command.

Never employ a deaf man or boy as a beater.

A retriever is very useful in covert-shooting, if used for retrieving only.

In large woods, when not shooting in battue, take every advantage of open places, and secure free scope for firing. Do not get under overhanging branches. The art of knowing where to place yourself for a favorable shot, is one of the secrets of success in covert-shooting.

And do not refuse fair chances, under the hope or impression of meeting with better ones.

In coverts, the paths or open passages are called rides; and lawns or openings in woods are termed glades.

After beating a covert, the adjoining and surrounding hedges, clumps, and bushes should be beaten. A very exciting finale to a day's sport may thus be obtained; particularly in pheasant-shooting.

When shooting in covert, employ plenty of dogs, for "many dogs find most game;" when rabbit-shooting, seek out a clear space of ground, of about ten square yards or more, and there stand as still as you can, and you will assuredly have a far better share of the sport than by roaming about with the dogs.

In no branch of the sport of shooting is there greater necessity for pointing out the perils attending it than in covert-shooting.

It must be distinctly impressed on the minds of persons going out with others in a covert, to keep in line; and never to shoot in any direction where you have the least suspicion another person may be. The danger is great in covers where the ground is upon a level, but it is increased on an undulated or hilly surface.

As another warning to my young friends, I add Captain Lacy's sad tale of the death of a youth who was accidentally killed by his companions whilst shooting in a covert. The captain says:

"To prove what even a single small shot-corn may do, we have an instance but too melancholy, where one of a party who had just been shooting in covert was missing, but was shortly afterwards found lying in a senseless state; nor could this for some time be accounted for by his mournful companions, till at last some one discovered a very small speck of blood just above the eyeball, where the pellet had entered and penetrated the brain. Slight as the injury externally appeared to be, it terminated fatally; and thus was a fine youth, an only child, and the sole heir to immense wealth, prematurely cut off—a case almost too afflicting to commemorate, further than as it may serve as a salutary warning to other shooters in covert, how guardedly cautious at all times they ought to be in observing the proper time and direction in which they may venture to fire with perfect safety."

THE DUTY OF BEATERS.

Though a sportsman is said to "beat" a field by simply running his dog over it in search of game, he himself is not a beater, in the term implied in sporting language.

A beater, strictly speaking, is one who accompanies the sportsman; and with a staff, beats the bushes, fences, covers, or whatever else may harbor the game: his object in beating being to turn it out into the "open," so that the sportsman may shoot it as it flies or runs, as the case may be.

The duty of beaters is therefore very simple, but differs according to the nature of the game, the country, the time of year, and other circumstances.

For instance, in a thick cover, when beating for pheasants or woodcocks, the more noise that is made the better; whilst, on the contrary, when beating for grouse, partridges, snipes, and such birds as are not in the habit of frequenting woods and thick coverts, but generally lie in low ground-cover, the beaters cannot be too silent: they should approach likely shots as noiselessly as possible, and then suddenly beat out the game.

The beater should never call out, on starting any thing in front of him; because the sportsman, if attending to his duty, is sure to see it. It is only in case of any thing turning back or going in a contrary direction that the beater should break silence; and then only by simply calling out "Back!" or "Behind!" and instantly jumping into the ditch to get out of the way, as he says the word.

The moment the sportsman has fired his gun, the beater should stand still, and encourage the dogs to do the like, whilst the gun is being reloaded; after which he may go and pick up the game.

On beating a wood, the beaters, who generally consist of two or more, should keep strictly in line as they pass through beating every bit of cover likely to harbor the game in pursuit: and on any one or more of the sportsmen discharging their guns, the whole line of beaters, as well as the sportsmen, should stand still, and not advance a step until the guns are all reloaded, and the signal given to "go on!"

On beating a fence, if only one beater, the sportsman should go on the opposite side; but taking care to keep in line with him. If there be a beater on each side of the fence, the same strictness as to keeping in line with each other must be observed.

9*

THE BATTUE.

Battue is a word derived from the French: literally, it is "bush-beating." But in this country it signifies a party of sportsmen beating a covert by walking in line, at equal distances apart, for the purpose of shooting game: a number of beaters and game gatherers following: generally one between each two sportsmen. And in this manner, hundreds of pheasants and hares are sometimes slaughtered in the space of a few hours. In preserves which are swarming with game, a battue certainly bears the aspect of wanton sport. Whenever a shot is fired by either of the party, the whole of the beaters and sportsmen halt in lines abreast, whilst the discharged gun is reloaded: and the success depends very much on the discipline and strict obedience of the sportsmen to this injunction.

It is a general rule at battue, that hen pheasants should be spared; and cocks only shot. And this rule also prevails in the Highlands as to grey-hens (the females of the black cock), which are always spared by sportsmen who advocate the increase of game.

In battue, whenever a hen rises, the signal "ware hen!" is called out by the sportsman or beater who is nearest it: meaning thereby "beware of the hen;" or, literally, "do not shoot the hen pheasant." In most places where game is very strictly preserved, and the rules of sporting firmly adhered to, a fine is imposed on any one who kills a hen pheasant in battue. And, according to the "Oakleigh shooting code," there are several other fines which are strictly enforced among sportsmen in North Staffordshire.

TABLE OF FINES PAYABLE ON OAKLEIGH MANOR, NORTH STAFFORDSHIRE.

	£	s.	d.
Killing a grey-hen or hen-pheasant . . .	0	2	6
For a second the same day . . .	0	7	6
For a third, fourth, fifth, &c., each .	0	10	0
Dropping two or more birds from one barrel . .	0	2	6
Shooting at black game, red-grouse, pheasants, or partridges on the ground	0	5	0
And for every bird so killed . . .	0	5	0
Killing a bird not in season . . .	0	5	0
Shooting at a bird not in season . .	0	2	6
Shooting at a hare (leverets allowed) between 10th February and 1st September . .	0	2	6
Shooting at a snipe between 10th February and 1st August	0	2	6

In some counties the fine for shooting a hen pheasant is half a guinea.

These fines are strictly insisted on in many places : they are handed over to the gamekeepers who belong to the estate.

No dogs need be used in battue, but beaters only: and it should be remembered that pheasants always run to the end or side of the cover before taking flight, unless they are much pressed: consequently the best sport always comes at the extreme end of the wood.

It is usual on the day or morning before a battue, to place nets about three or four feet high, at intervals, and round the further end, side, and boundaries of the covert, in order to prevent the pheasants from running out; which numbers of them would otherwise do. On reaching the net, after attempting to get through, they run back in the direction of the beaters, and are then compelled to fly. The best shooting always takes place at the end of the covert; where, being . driven into close quarters, the birds are at last obliged to take to their wings. Without nets few shots only could be had; but immense slaughter may be made by preventing the pheasants running out of the covert.

When getting near the end of a wood which has been closely beaten, the two outside sportsmen should go forward and stand perfectly still, keeping a sharp look out. There are almost sure to be some skulkers reluctant to leave their retreat. On these occasions pheasants often squat in the last clump of thick bushes; which they will not quit until hard pressed.

After a battue, always beat the boundary fences and adjacent hedgerows. Good clear shots may thus be obtained.

Only two or three battues are allowed in the course of the year in any one covert, where the proprietor wishes to keep up his preserves. Pheasants would forsake the cover if too often subject to these terrific onslaughts.

At battues it is by no means unusual for each sportsman to be attended by his own servant, whose duty it is to keep a score of all the game his master kills; and as three or four guns are sometimes fired at the same bird, by different sportsmen within range; and as each person who fires claims the credit of killing, and directs his servant to score accordingly, at the end of the day's sport it is found there are very many more birds scored than can be found in the game-bag.

Some gentlemen, proprietors of game preserves,

who have a motive or whim in making an exaggerated return of the abundance of game on their preserves, shut their eyes to such inaccuracies, and take pleasure in sending to the press a report of the number of head of game killed on a certain day. In many instances these reports, being taken from the individual scoring cards of each sportsman, are grossly inaccurate ; and sometimes double the number of head actually bagged, are put down as killed.

A *breech-loader* is the best sort of gun for a battue, because of the rapidity with which shots may be had, particularly on arriving at an extremity of the cover, where the nets prevent the pheasants from running out; and they then rise up in such numbers that a quick succession of shots may be made by an active sportsman.

SNIPE-SHOOTING.

This sport may very justly be termed the zenith of the art of shooting flying. It is the truest test of good shooting; none but good shots are able to make up a bag, or kill their ten couple of snipes in a day. Bad shots and young sportsmen fire away pounds of ammunition at snipes without touching a feather. In the *jack snipes* they are sorely puzzled; in the *common* or *whole snipe*, they find their match.

The most skilful sportsmen often miss them; though when well practised at snipes, more than at any other objects of the gun, a good shot kills almost every one he fires at.

It is a sport peculiar in itself, for it may be had in all quarters of the globe; but it is one that requires considerable practice, with some knowledge of their habits, and also of the mode of searching for them. And to my mind they are well worth the trouble; for a snipe, though but a mouthful, is one of the choicest of tid-bits that is brought to the breakfast table.

Activity in the movements of the body, with steadiness in handling the gun, and a quick and accurate eye, are among the first essentials in the snipe shot.

Snipes arrive during the latter part of September, and in October; but in much larger numbers in November and December.

They generally lie better during windy weather than at any other time; and by reason of their flying against wind on being disturbed, they are a steadier and easier mark for the sportsman then than on other occasions.

They are puzzling to the sportsman on bright cheerful days, and during white frosts, by reason of the greater vigilance and activity which they display.

It is an error to suppose that the slightest touch of the shot will bring them down. It depends entirely upon where the shot strikes. Their bones are very small and delicate, and their feathers very penetrable, therefore one pellet of No. 8 or 9 shot may sometimes break a wing or strike in a vital part; in either case the bird must fall. But a snipe will sometimes fly away with three or four shot in its body.

The general reason why young sportsmen miss snipes is, because they shoot neither forward enough nor high enough. They are such extremely active birds on wing, that a slow or careless shot stands a poor chance of killing them.

I recommend a breech-loader for snipe-shooting, for the reasons stated at page 52. When snipes are abundant, it is a common occurrence for some to get up whilst the sportsman is reloading. Rapidity of loading is, therefore, of great consideration is snipe-shooting. And, as snipe-walks are generally very wet, the annoyance of placing the but-end of your gun on the ground to reload is avoided with a breech-loader.

Shot of the size No. 7 or 8 is best for snipe-shooting.

When a snipe crosses either to right or left be sure to shoot well in advance; and, if a long shot, a foot or more is not an inch too much.

If the bird rises at thirty yards distance, knock it down as soon as possible, and before it commences those graceful evolutions which have so frequently been the theme of admiration.

But when snipes rise at your feet, or within twenty yards, give them more time; and the unsteady flight with which they start off will have settled into a quieter motion of the wings; and the sportsmen will thereby make a surer mark, and be more likely to bring his bird to bag.

But it is only when they lie well, and rise within a short distance, that they can be allowed to complete their zigzags; the greater number of shots, it will be found, must be made in double-quick time.

When looking for snipes, walk steadily and silently; with the eye ranging well in advance.

Always work *down wind* when in search of snipes; because, on being disturbed, they fly up wind, and so pass to the right or left of the sportsman, within fair range. If the sportsman proceeds in a contrary direction, so rapidly does the snipe fly from him, that it is out of range before he can accurately level his gun.

A pointer or setter may be easily trained to stand at snipes, and an active dog so trained is of great service in snipe-shooting; but by reason of the necessity of going down wind whenever you can, the dog should be taught to hunt at right angles to the wind. When the dog stands, make a circle, and head him from the leewardmost position.

Snipes do not lie about frozen places; they may be found in small rivulets and unfrozen waters, in dykes, bogs, and marshes, during frosty weather.

The most unlikely time to find snipes in their usual haunts is during a white frost; on occasions of the kind they assemble in "wisps," and take to the uplands, and on being disturbed spring altogether.

In cloudy, threatening weather, and sometimes on warm days, snipes lie close; and on being disturbed, fly with less activity, and altogether in a steadier and lazier manner; on such occasions they are easy to shoot.

Jack snipes always lie close, especially in long

grass, from which they will not rise without very close beating; and then they are so foolish as to pitch again and again within one hundred yards of the same spot; and sometimes giving the bad shot six or seven chances ere they can be frightened far from their haunts.

Day after day the same jack snipes may be found in the same walks and the same spots; and day by day the novice may fire away at them to no purpose; for though they rise at his feet, he constantly misses them; and so, a couple of jack snipes may afford him a week's sport ere he brings them to the bag; indeed such is no uncommon occurrence.

Young sportsmen frequently fancy from these birds pitching again so soon, that they are wounded; and he rushes forward under an impression that the bird will "never rise again." His delusion, however, soon subsides, as the tortuous little creature darts off again another hundred yards, and so on, working its young persecutor into a state of great excitement.

> "So swift a bird is apt to make
> Young shots with indecision shake;
> Such are indebted when they kill
> Much more to fortune than to skill."

The common snipe is an extremely watchful bird:

and a sportsman must tread the marsh lightly as a
fairy, if he hopes to get within point blank range
of it.

On heaths and rush-clad hills, and in turnip fields,
they are less exposed and less difficult of approach.

The chances are twenty to one against a novice
killing a common snipe.

The great snipe is by no means a difficult bird to
kill ; not only on account of its larger size, but because
of its steadier flight and more sluggish habits. It
generally lies well, and offers a fair chance to the
sportsman. They are, however, scarce birds, but delicious morsels.

A keen-eyed sportsman distinguishes its species the
moment it rises from the ground, by reason of its red
tail and heavy body, with white in the under part.
When disturbed, they generally pitch again within a
very short distance.

All snipes are uncertain in their movements. Whenever good sport is had, it is generally unexpectedly :
and *vice versâ*, sometimes when the weather appears
to be exactly suited for finding them in certain haunts,
the sportsman is disappointed. Therefore when plenty
of snipes are found, make the most of your sport.
One frosty night will drive them from their haunts.

In boisterous weather, snipes are more scattered about the walks. It is in frosty weather and bright sunny days that they are more frequently seen in wisps.

On shooting a snipe, keep your eye on the spot where it falls, or carefully mark it by some conspicuous object, whilst reloading: a dead or wounded snipe is sometimes difficult to find. If it falls into the water, wipe the feathers dry before putting it in your pocket.

If you are a very quick shot, and can handle your gun dexterously, you will never do wrong by shooting at a snipe the moment it rises to the level of your shoulder: that is to say, whenever it gets up at thirty yards' distance and upwards. The snipe has neither way nor speed upon it at first, and is as steady a mark as can be desired at the moment alluded to: but after flying about twenty paces it is at the top of its speed. Therefore, when snipes are wild, knock them down whilst they cry " scaipe !" or rather " schayich !" which they generally do as they spring from the bog.

December is always the best month for snipe-shooting, particularly if no severe frosts prevail.

THE FLIGHT OF SNIPES.

The flight of these birds is swift, graceful, and beautiful in the extreme. There is no bird whose flight is more to be admired. Sportsmen gaze at them with pleasure; whilst the naturalist beholds them with curious admiration, as they gracefully whirl through the air in semicircular ascent; after performing the prettiest and most perfect flittings, alternately to right and left, as if to gather speed as a skater, wherewith to assist in more elegant evolutions. The snipe, like the skater, then glances off into an elliptical gyration; and then, after five or ten minutes' performance in the air, often drops again within a few yards of the same spot as that from whence it sprang; but sometimes running a few yards after alighting.

On rising from the ground, a snipe starts with a rapid zigzag motion; darting off with powerful strokes of its wings a few yards; and then, raising its head as if to look around, steadily soars, and commences a tortuous line of flight. It is just at the finish of its twistings, and at the commencement of its curvilinear course, that it offers the best mark to the sportsman;

but, as it is very often out of range before the zigzag performances are concluded, it will not always be prudent to wait for the better chance, but rather try your skill at the bird in its most puzzling form of flight.

On warm, windy, and cloudy days, snipes fly with lazier and more careless effort than on bright or frosty days.

It is the common snipe which is the most active and vigilant in all its motions, and consequently the most difficult to kill. The large snipe is not so wild: though in the motion of its wings, the form and line of flight resemble the other; still it is less rapid and tortuous. On rising from the mire, the large snipe often soars up perpendicularly in the air several yards; so that, when flushed at the feet of the sportsman, the bird seems to soar directly over his head.

The flight of the jack snipe is similar to the large snipe, with the exception that it never soars high in the air on first springing from the ground; and very seldom performs any of those elliptical evolutions so much admired in the common snipe.

Some sportsmen, good shots in other respects, do not shoot at snipes, because of the difficulty they experience in hitting them.   The fact is, they have never carefully watched and considered the flight of the snipe, in its varied and beautiful gyrations, or they might kill them as certainly as they do any other birds.

HARES.

I am one of those who consider hares ought never to be shot; they cannot fairly be looked upon as legitimate objects of the sportsman's gun, but are the indisputable animals of the courser's chase.

> "And let the courser and the hunter share
>   Their just and proper title to the hare.
>   *   *   *   *
>   The tracing hound by nature was designed
>   Both for the use and pleasure of mankind;
>   Form'd for the hare, the hare too for the hound,
>   In enmity each to each other bound."

Foxes have a passport which holds them free from harm, though they run the gauntlet of a thousand guns; and why should not the same privilege be granted to the hare?

When a hare jumps off its form, within range of the gun, it is so fair a mark that it can seldom be missed by the most juvenile of sportsmen; and if not killed, is almost certain to be wounded.

In order to kill a hare on the spot, at a reasonable distance, running straight away, the gun should be levelled at the tips of the ears, if they are standing; but if the ears are thrown back on the shoulders, the aim should be just over the forehead, and slightly in advance of the nose. If young sportsmen would only remember this when wishing to shoot a hare running from them, they would never fail to kill on the spot, at any distance between twenty-five and forty yards. Observing that the greater the distance, the higher and more advanced must be the aim.

In shooting at a hare running across to right or left, aim well in advance; and if far off, as high as the tips of the ears would be if erect.

When the hare is running across ploughed or ridged land, be careful to fire as it rises to the crown of the ridge; not whilst dipping its head in the furrow. Unless this is attended to, the chances of killing are very remote. In shooting at a hare in turnips or mangold, fire well in advance, or you will not kill her.

The remark made elsewhere in these pages, that a bird may be killed at a greater distance when crossing than when running from or approaching the

10

sportsman, applies with equal force to hares and rabbits; which may sometimes be killed ten or twenty yards further in cross than in straight-away shots.

When the sportsman sees a hare approaching him, he should stand as motionless as possible until it is abroad-side, and then fire as soon as practicable, and according to the rules before laid down; bearing in mind the necessity of regulating his aim according to distance.

Use No. 4 shot for a hare; and do not fire at too great or doubtful distances.

In a neighborhood where hares are not much hunted, they lie very close on open fields, and often get up at the feet of the sportsman; on such occasions they jump off their form, and then run at a tremendous pace; but when much hunted, they become less trustful, and steal off slyly on suspicion of danger, running away at the top of their speed.

In stubble and fallow fields, hares generally lie within a range of thirty or forty yards from the hedge. Those are the favorite and most likely distances at which to find a hare, be the size of the field what it may.

In wet weather hares prefer high ground. In dry

THE CAPPING, OR TUBING POSITION.

weather they lie most in the valleys and lowlands. But they are sometimes very uncertain, and where you feel almost sure of finding a hare, you find, instead, an empty form.

Before seating itself, and particularly after having been chased by dogs, a hare will sometimes take a long leap into its form, so as to cut of the scent.

As a general rule, the further a hare is found from any covert, the better it will run ; it shows the greater confidence in its speed.

The favorite outlying places of a hare are wheat-stubbles, fallows, clover, and grass-lands.

When a hare is chased by a dog across a fallow, it will assuredly turn into a furrow, ere it proceeds far across the ridges.

RABBIT-SHOOTING.

If not good sport, this is unquestionably capital fun. Young sportsmen are particularly fond of it; and it is very good practice, teaching them to " look sharp," and be quick in handling the gun.

As this sport is pursued with much greater zeal by young sportsmen than by old ones, it is necessary to warn the inexperienced of the dangers attending it, and to remind them that many deplorable accidents have arisen through the indiscretion and over-eager. ness of young rabbit-shooters.

There is one universal rule in this sport which should be strictly observed from one end of the land to the other, which is this :

" Beware of shooting at a rabbit in the hedge." Though ever so fair a chance offers, and though you may feel certain there is no one on the other side of the fence, make it a rule through life, never, *under any circumstancees*, to fire at any thing, whether rabbit, bird, or otherwise, in the hedge. Though the chances be ever so inviting, and your confidence ever so great, do not for the sake of killing a paltry little creature, incur the risk of killing, maiming, or blinding for life, a human being, a horse, a cow, or some other valuable animal which may be on the other side of the bushes.

All experienced sportsmen are so extremely tenacious on this point, that if they saw a fellow-sportsman infringe it, they would never again go out with him so long as he carried a gun. And I have seen an old sportsman take a gun from a youth who shot a rabbit whilst it was running along the hedge, box his ears, and send him off home, with a prohibition that he should never again bring a gun upon his estate.

Those only who have seen narrow escapes (as I have), can truly estimate the importance of a firm ad-herence, through life, to this simple rule, "Never shoot at any thing in a hedge." A disregard of it has embittered with sorrow the cup of life of many a father, brother, friend, and near and dear relative.

> "Ye parents, let your sons these stories know,
> And thus you may prevent the distant woe."

> "Such sad events in every place have been,
> Such fatal ends have darkened every scene."

Rabbits are among the most prolific animals in the world. Daniel, in his "Rural Sports," says: "they breed at six months old, bear seven times annually, and bring five young ones each time."

It is therefore very easy to get up a rabbit war-ren anywhere, and in a very short time.

Rabbit-shooting in a covert, where here and there a clear plot of ground can be found, is lively sport; and it is the same in parks, and on heath-land, where there are extensive beds of fern and furze. Rides should be cut and cleared through it, and then capi-tal snap-shooting may be had.

For rabbit-shooting, plenty of small dogs are required, to scuttle about the bushes and thickets, to turn the rabbits out; for they sometimes require a great deal of pressing before they will quit their hiding-places.

The sportsman should stand perfectly still and silent whilst his dogs are hunting, keep a vigilant lookout on the clear space of ground in front of him; and on the rabbits crossing it, which they are sure to do when hard pressed, he will find it capital fun to knock them over. Shoot well in advance, aiming just in front of bunnie's nose, and you may be sure of killing. Fix your eye on the head of the rabbit, as if that were the only vulnerable part.

The thick fur coat of a rabbit is a powerful resister to shot; and unless the shot strikes a vital part, there is no certainty of killing a rabbit beyond thirty-five yards' distance. A small light gun will do for rabbit-shooting; and the best sized shot is No. 5.

Rabbits are very active and tenacious of life. Unless hit severely, they are sure to get away, and crawl into a burrow and die.

Calm, fine weather is best for the sport. Cold north winds are always unfavorable.

As soon as ever the rabbit is clear of the fence or thicket (if at a reasonable distance), the sportsman should shoot. Take the first chance, for it is seldom a second offers.

On warm, sunny days, when rabbits lie out, they are more fond of lying in tufts of grass than in any thing else. They are generally pretty close to the hedge, and will assuredly make for it on being started.

Be careful not to shoot the dog instead of the rabbit. All dogs have a strong propensity for chasing rabbits, and run after them with their noses close to the scut. Whenever a dog is very close upon the rabbit, the sportsman should never shoot; unless, in his cruelty, he had rather kill or blind the dog, than shoot the rabbit.

Snap-shooting to perfection may be had with rabbits in a low cover up which a ride is cut and cleared. One side of it should be hunted at a time; and so, after all the rabbits are driven across the ride from one cover, they can be beaten back again, and so made to run the gauntlet a second time. In order to become a good snap-shot, a man must have a very quick, ready hand, and a watchful eye.

Ferreting rabbits is slow sport compared with the other; though sometimes, when they "bolt well," it is very good fun. Choose a calm sunny day for ferreting. Keep your tongue quiet and stand still, but never in front of a hole. If a rabbit comes to the mouth of the burrow, and sees a dog or a man in front, it is ten to one but it will retreat. But where strict silence is observed, and every one keeps in his place, the rabbit will steal out, pause, look around, and then dart off at the top of its speed.

When a ferret lays up, the best mode of drawing it is, to rip open the belly of a newly-killed rabbit and thrust it into the hole on the windward side of the burrow; the fumes of the warm entrails are generally irresistible to the ferret, and draw it, as if by magic, to the scent.

Excellent practice with the pea-rifle may be had, on summer evenings, by hiding within range of a spot where rabbits creep out to feed. A meadow, or park skirting a wood, is exceedingly favorable for this sport.

The months of December and January afford the favorite time and season for rabbit-shooting and fer-reting.

A FEW STRAY HINTS.

NEVER put a ramrod down an empty barrel after the gun has been discharged; because it loosens adhering substances, which block up the nipples, and cause a mis-fire.

If your shooting-ground lies at a distance from home, always let your dogs ride there; and the same on returning.

Do not toil too hard at the sport, particularly if you are not very strong. Over-exertion weakens the nerves and injures the constitution.

The sportsman, during the month of September, should never take the field without a knife, a drinking-horn, and a shilling for largesse.

By keeping a few of the most central fields on your manor quiet, and seldom or ever shooting in them, you have always a nursery to which your frightened birds will resort; and your stock of game will be maintained.

Always allow game to cool thoroughly before packing it; or you may have the mortification of

10*

receiving an acknowledgment from your friends at a distance, of a hamper of game, which arrived " *un peu trop haut.*"

Always hang up your birds in the larder by the legs, with their heads downwards, if you wish to keep them.

Game will not keep if carried long in the pocket; make your gillie carry them suspended by their necks, in a game-bag of net-work.

A hare will keep longer, and be of much nicer flavor, if paunched on the day it is shot; and before being hung up in the larder.

If game-birds remain a few hours packed in a hamper along with an unpaunched hare, they soon become tainted.

Never press the trigger unless certain that your aim is true; and never vary your eye from the bird you first fix upon as the object of your aim.

When a sportsman misses several shots in succession with one barrel, without being able to assign any reason for so doing, he should use the other exclusively for some time.

When a sportsman is fatigued or flurried, the arm and hand, and consequently the nerves, are never steady.

The young sportsman must always shun spirits;

the old one sometimes requires a stimulus of the kind to help him over the hedges, and to lift his legs out of the heavy soil fallows.

In shooting with a young sportsman, or a stranger, always allow him to precede you in getting over the fences: it may be that you save your life, or a limb, by the precaution.

Always correct and point out errors which you observe in young sportsmen; and rebuke any one, whether old or young, in whom you detect carelessness in handling the gun.

If, being no sportsman yourself, you invite one or two friends to shoot over your manor, do not offer or propose to "walk with them." Sportsmen always enjoy the sport more if *unaccompanied* by the nonsporting friend who invites them. But do not forget to send them a luncheon. Very hard toil sometimes belongs to shooting; and sportsmen, generally, have keen appetites.

However generously disposed you may be towards your friends and neighbors, if you have a valuable dog, never lend it: and the same may be said of a favorite gun. If your friend or neighbor thinks you unkind in refusing to lend either, show him this page in the book of the "Dead Shot."

PIGEON-SHOOTING.

PIGEON-SHOOTING is, unquestionably, the finest practice for the aspirant to excellence, in the use of the
gun at flying objects, of any that is used. At the
same time it is a sport which requires considerable
skill; and there is none in which so much depends
on the perfect coolness and steady deliberation of the
shooter. In no branch of our art are the nerves of
the shooter so severely tried, and so likely to be disturbed, as in a public shooting-match : though a great
deal of the trepidation may be quelled by frequent
practice.

I have seen many persons who are dead shots in
the field, completely eclipsed by very inferior sportsmen at a pigeon-match; and this entirely because
the nerves of the one were so much quieter and under
better control than the other.

The practitioner would do well, before shooting in
public, to practise several times previously, by himself,
far away from the gaze and observation of others.

With but few exceptions, a good shot, accustomed

to game in its wildest nature, is generally a good pigeon-shooter. But it is not so often the case, that a town pigeon-shot is equally skilful in shooting game; though in a majority of instances that have come under my observation, I have found really good town pigeon-match-shooters dead shots in the field, at game of all kinds.

The most difficult and brilliant part of the practice, is that in which two birds are released at the same instant, and sometimes from the same trap; double-barrelled guns being used. Such is, truly, a splendid test of the skill and dexterity of a sportsman. The usual distance at which the shooter stands from the traps, in double shooting, is twenty-one yards; and even at that short distance, he must be very quick with his first bird, or the second will be out of range before he can bring his gun to bear upon it, so powerful and rapid is the flight of the blue rock.

The proceedings at a shooting-match should always be conducted honorably and impartially: five traps are generally used; these are placed, each about five yards apart, in a semicircle in front of the shooter, at a distance from the measured standing place or "foot-mark," varying from twenty to forty yards, according to the skill of the shooter or the terms of the match.

The object of five traps, is simply to deceive the shooter as to the exact spot from whence the bird will rise; and with that view, birds are placed in all five traps, before the sportsman takes his stand at the foot-mark.

Prizes of guns, rifles, gold and silver cups, and tankards are frequently contended for; and sometimes prizes in money, sweepstakes, and handicaps, which are raised by the competitors subscribing each £1 or £5 as may be agreed on; and the greater the number of subscribers the higher the stakes; which in this instance are generally divided into one, two, or three prizes. The best shot has the first or highest prize, the second best the second prize, and so on.

As may be supposed, ties very frequently arise in the shooting; that is to say, two or more of the shooters kill an equal number of birds; in which case the competitors who tie, shoot again; each, bird for bird, until one or other of the party misses, and then withdraws; and when the ties are reduced to two competitors only, the two continue shooting alternately until one misses his bird; the one who shoots all the ties without missing, then ranks first; the one who kept it up second best, ranks second, and so on, according to the number of prizes.

Guns of rather larger calibre than those used for partridge-shooting are generally employed in pigeon-shooting: the customary gauge of a pigeon gun is No. 12, and none larger than No. 10 should be permitted.

There is no restriction as to powder, but the usual charge is, from $2\frac{3}{4}$ to three drachms; that of shot from 1 oz. to $1\frac{1}{2}$ oz.; and the size of the shot No. 5 or No. 6. Nos. 7 and 8 are sometimes used, but these will not do in a brisk wind. It is important that all competitors should use the same-sized shot; and therefore it is usual for all to load from the same bowl, any size and charge of shot agreed on.

It is usual at pigeon-matches to stipulate that the shooter be allowed to use a larger charge of shot than the maximum quantity, on having the distance at which he shoots increased, at the rate of one yard for every one-eighth of an ounce of extra shot.

The blue-rock pigeons are those generally used at shooting matches, because they are the strongest fliers and hardest diers; and they are, besides, the nearest approach to wild pigeons; which are well known as such extraordinary birds for flying off unharmed from a heavy charge of shot.

When the competitors are numerous, six birds only

are allowed to each person : but where they are few, it is usual for each competitor to be allowed ten or a dozen birds. The pigeons should all be of the same quality and color, and taken without choice, no person being allowed to select his own birds.

At 21 yards rise, the boundary fence should be 80 yards from the traps. Beyond that rise, the boundary should be 100 yards.

The best and most durable traps for pigeon-shooting are made of iron; these, on being pulled, rattle most and frighten the bird up. The iron pigeon trap is usually about twelve inches square (or twelve inches by ten). To the bottom, or floor of the trap, are attached two half tubes, placed longitudinally, so as to raise it about three inches from the ground. There is also a small hole in the floor, through which an iron pin is driven, in order to hold it firmly to the ground. The four sides and top of the trap are all joined together by easy working hinges; and the aft side is also joined by hinges to the floor of the trap. The front side has two or three loop-holes to admit light, and induce the bird to stand with its tail towards the shooter. On the top or crown of the trap is a circular hole, about four inches in diameter, which closes with a lid and clasp. This hole is merely for

the purpose of putting the bird in, after the trap is
fairly fixed and ready. The cord by which the trap
is pulled, is fastened to an iron loop on the top-front
hinge; consequently, the top and four sides of the
trap may be all pulled over by one cord, in an instant; and on falling backwards, they open and lie
flat on the ground.

The iron trap described, is such as is used at the
Hornsey Wood House shooting grounds, the Red
House, Battersea, and other distinguished match-
shooting localities.

Wooden traps are seldom used now at public
shooting grounds, except for sparrow and starling-
shooting.

The term "H and T" traps, refers merely to tossing (head or tail) for choice of two traps, which are
placed one to the right and the other to the left of
the shooter. And this is a very customary proceeding in pigeon-shooting, particularly when two traps
only are used; it insures fairness, and is a check upon
the trapper, who may have put a strong bird in one
trap and a weak one in the other.

More than a little skill and dexterity are required
in pulling the trap: and for that reason none but
those experienced in the art are chosen to perform so

important a duty. There is plenty of room for fraud and collusion in pulling the trap, consequently a trustworthy person should be appointed puller. For instance, he might pull the trap so gently for one competitor as to raise it only a few inches, and thereby permit the bird to glide off several yards before the shooter sees it. And, on the other hand, in case he wanted to favor any particular shooter, he would pull the trap suddenly and sharply (which is the fair way), and then the bird flies up perpendicularly, directly in front of the shooter, and so offers a fair chance.

When the match is between two persons only, it is sometimes stipulated that each shall act as puller to the other. The usual plan is, for each to find a trap and trapper for the other, and such is considered the fairest proceeding; for there is also room for fraud and collusion with the trapper, as to supplying strong birds to one person and weak ones to another; and as to pulling feathers out of their wings, and so impeding their flight.

Sometimes, but not usually, it is stipulated that each shooter shall gather his own birds. Much . time, however, is saved by appointing a gatherer for all parties.

Handicapping, according to skill and past performances in pigeon-shooting, is a difficult and delicate task ; it should always be performed with discretion, and the handicapper appointed unanimously.

The term "fair bird," in pigeon-shooting, implies a bird which rises fairly, and may be shot at whilst on the wing.

"Dead bird," implies a bird fairly risen, shot, and gathered within range.

"Lost bird," is that which is shot at and missed ; also any bird which, after being wounded, falls without the boundary.

"No bird," when through some mistake or accident, the bird was not risen according to the rules ; or when the shooter had no fair chance, and, consequently, is entitled to another in its stead.

The young pigeon-shot will do well to consider attentively the lessons on the art of shooting which have been given in preceding pages, and which apply with equal force to shooting pigeons as to shooting game ; bearing in mind that it is necessary to aim well in advance of a fast bird, going right or left ; and over its back, on going straight away.

Professional pigeon-shooters acquire a habit of killing their birds the moment they are out of the trap ; and some of these men often kill nineteen birds out of twenty, with splendid precision, at twenty-five yards' rise. The knack of killing them in this manner consists in taking them the instant they rise, and being cautious not to fire too low ; remembering that they are rising, not flying forward.

It may be worth while to caution the inexperienced against being drawn into a match with "professional pigeon-shooters," some of whom, I am sorry to say, are mere "professional cheats."

They generally stipulate that each person shall find his own trap ; and among their contrivances for unfair advantage, is that of using a "spring trap," which is neither more nor less than a "cheating trap." In appearance it resembles an ordinary pigeon trap, but it contains an ingeniously contrived spring, which, on the trap being pulled, causes the bird to fly in a particular direction, such as the "professional" is most practised in shooting ; and so he seldom fails to kill his bird.

And they sometimes induce country sportsmen to shoot a pigeon-match with them, without any stipulation as to guns or shot; and then, perhaps, on coming to the ground, where the sportsman expects to meet his opponents on equal terms, and he is provided with a gun of No. 12 calibre, they have guns of No.

6 gauge! from which they fire four or five drachms of powder, and two ounces or more of shot!

Another of their well-known but more recent contrivances is, that of using loaded waddings: these, to all appearances, are mere thick paper waddings; but on opening them, they will be found each to contain nearly a quarter of an ounce of shot.

There are many other equally disgraceful tricks which are sometimes resorted to by " professionals ;" and I need scarcely say, that such are the practices which bring pigeon-shooting into disrepute.

For these reasons gentlemen-sportsmen generally refuse to shoot with strangers, lest they should be " professional tricksters."

Strange to say, until the publication of the first edition of this work, there were no other printed or authorized rules in regard to pigeon-shooting, than those of the old Battersea school; and though some of those are useful, they are quite inadequate to the requirements of the present day. In the event of any difficulty or dispute arising at a shooting-match, it has been usual to refer the matter to the editors of " Bell's Life in London," whose decisions thereon have generally been sound and good.

Now, as many thousands of pigeon-shooting match-

es take place every year in the country, and the absence and want of an authorized code of laws by
which to regulate the shooting, and conduct these
matches satisfactorily, has frequently been felt, and
to my own knowledge has too often been the cause
of painful disputes, I carefully prepared a concise list
of rules, which were submitted to and approved by
some of the most experienced pigeon-shots in London,
and which I trust have been found to meet the wants
which were so long felt in the conduct of shooting-
matches.

MARKSMAN'S RULES.

1. Before subscribers' names are entered and
stakes received, the following preliminaries should
be arranged, viz. : the number of birds to be allowed
to each person; the number of traps to be employed ;
the distance at which the birds are to be risen; the
boundary within which they must fall; the size of
shot, and weight or measure of a charge; all which
should be put down in writing, and signed by the
subscribers.

2. Before the match commences, a scorer, a trapper, a puller, two umpires, and a referee must be
chosen; also one or more gatherers; and if a gatherer

is to be allowed the assistance of a dog, it should be so stipulated. The referee must be mutually chosen, and the umpires, one by each party; each party may also appoint a puller, or they may both agree to the same puller.

3. All disputes to be settled by the umpires, and in case they cannot agree, the decision of the referee to be final.

4. No gun to be used exceeding in calibre the gauge No. 10. The maximum charges of shot to be $1\frac{1}{8}$ oz., $1\frac{1}{4}$ oz., or $1\frac{1}{2}$ oz., *as the case may be;* all charges of shot to be measured or weighed, and guns loaded, in presence of the umpires and referee. In single-bird shooting, when both barrels are allowed to each bird, the size of the gun should not exceed No. 12 gauge, and the charge of shot must be limited to $1\frac{1}{4}$ oz.

5. Each competitor must hold himself in readiness, and come to the foot-mark on his name being called by the scorer; it being at the discretion of the umpires and referee as to whether an absentee may be permitted to shoot after the lapse of ten minutes from the time he is called to the foot-mark.

6. Any competitor may challenge another, as to any suspected unfairness in loading; and the person

challenged must draw his charge of shot, or permit it to be drawn, in presence of the umpires; when, if it is found to exceed the maximum allowance, the person challenged is to pay a fine of £1 to the sweepstakes or prize fund, and be disqualified for shooting in the match or sharing in the result. But if the charge of shot be found not to exceed the fair maximum allowance, then the challenger to pay a forfeit of 2s. 6d. to the party challenged.

7. Any person challenged to pay a fine of 10s. to the prize fund or stakes, if he fires his gun off before the charge has been drawn and weighed, or measured, as the case may be.

8. The use of one barrel only [*or both, as the case may be*] to be allowed to each bird. If the match is for double shots, *i. e.*, at two birds to be risen at the same time; if the shooter miss with his first barrel, he is at liberty to shoot with his second barrel at the same bird.

9. The shooter, when ready, to say "pull!" and the puller to receive and obey such as the signal to pull the trap fairly over, and release the bird *instanter*.

10. After the shooter has taken his stand at the foot-mark, he is not to level his gun, or raise the but-

end above his elbow, until the bird is on the wing. On any competitor infringing this rule, the bird will be scored against him as a "lost bird," whether he kills it or not.

11. If the trap be pulled, or the bird released before, or not at the time of the signal, the shooter to have the option of calling "no bird!" and refusing to shoot: but if he shoots, the bird will be deemed a "fair one," and scored for or against him as the result may be.

12. If the bird does not rise immediately after the trap is pulled, the shooter to have the option of calling "no bird!" but if he shoots on its afterwards rising, it will be considered a "fair bird." If he advances beyond the foot-mark, shoots at the bird on the trap, or on the ground, before it rises, it will be scored against him as a "lost bird;" and this whether he kills it or not.

13. A bird must be shot whilst on the wing, in order to score as a "fair bird" (*with this exception only*),—that when both barrels are allowed to each bird, and the shooter having wounded a bird with his first barrel, the second may be fired at the bird on the ground, if the shooter fears it may rise again or escape beyond the boundary before it can be gathered.

11

14. If after giving the signal "pull!" the gun should be found uncapped, without a tube, or improperly loaded; or if the shooter, through negligence, is unable to fire, and the bird flies away, it will be scored against him as a "lost bird."

15. But in case of a mis-fire, through the cap or tube not exploding, or failing to ignite the charge, or other accidental circumstance not attributable to the shooter's negligence, he may call "no bird!" and claim another.

16. In single-bird matches, if two or more birds be liberated at the same time (whether accidentally or otherwise), the shooter to have the option of calling "no bird!" and refusing to shoot at either; but if he shoots, the bird will be scored for or against him, as the result may be.

17. And in double-bird matches, if more than two birds be liberated at the same time, the shooter may kill as many as he can; and all he kills within the boundary shall be scored in his favor; or he may refuse to fire at either, and claim two or more; but if he shoots at one or more, it will be scored as a "fair double shot," for or against him, as the case may be.

18. Whether a "fair bird," "dead bird," "lost

bird," or "no bird," must be decided in every case, during the match, by the umpires; and in case of dispute, the decision of the referee to be final.

19. Every bird must be gathered within the boundary, in order to score as "a dead bird."

20. Any bird which, after being shot at, perches or settles on the top of the boundary fence, is to be deemed a "lost bird;" and if, after perching or settling on the boundary fence, it falls or returns back within the boundary, it is nevertheless to be considered a "lost bird;" because it has been out of the boundary by alighting upon it. So also if it perches or settles on a tree or building within the boundary, whether it afterwards falls or not, it is a "lost bird;" because the probability is, that but for the tree or building, the bird would have had strength left to have flown out of bounds.

21. If a bird, after being fairly shot at, strikes against the fence, and then falls within the bounary and is gathered, it will be scored in favor of the shooter as a "dead bird."

22. If a bird be shot at and hit so hard by the shooter, that in the opinion of the umpires it would have fallen within bounds, but before falling was shot by a scout or some other person, it will be

deemed "no bird," and the shooter may claim another. But if in the opinion of the umpires the bird was missed, or only slightly wounded by the shooter, and afterwards killed by the scout within bounds, it is in that case to be scored against the shooter as a "lost bird."

23. When H and T traps are employed, a bird must always be put in each trap before the toss.

24. When a competitor allows his opponent any extra number of birds, the opponent so favored, to have the option of shooting them at the beginning or close of the contest.

25. Any competitor wilfully interrupting another whilst at the foot-mark, to pay a fine of £1 to the stakes or prize fund, and be disqualified for shooting and sharing in the results of the match; and the shooter so interrupted to have the option of calling "no bird!" and claiming another, whether he shoots during the interruption or not.

26. Any competitor using loaded waddings, or by any other device putting more shot or lead into the gun than the stipulated quantum, to pay a fine of £1 to the stakes or prize fund, and be disqualified for shooting or sharing in the results of the match.

27. In a shooting-match, all ties to be shot off on the same ground, immediately after the match, if they can be concluded before sunset; but any competitor may refuse to shoot after sunset; and in case of such refusal, the tie-shooting to be completed on the next day, or on some other day appointed by the umpires and referee.

28. The ties in sweepstakes or prize shooting may agree to share or divide the stakes or prize: but if one or more of the ties refuse to share, it must be shot off.

29. Any one of the ties being absent, or not coming to the foot-mark to shoot off his tie within ten minutes after his name is called, on the same or an appointed day, to forfeit all claim to the sweepstakes or prize.

30. Any competitor or other person bribing or attempting to bribe the trapper or puller, or obtaining or attempting to obtain an unfair advantage in any way whatever, or wilfully infringing any or either of these rules, to pay a fine of £1 to the stakes or prize fund, and be disqualified for shooting or sharing in the results of the match.

STARLING AND SPARROW-SHOOTING.

For starling and sparrow-shooting-matches the same rules apply. But the rise for these should not exceed twenty or twenty-one yards : as sparrows and small birds cannot be killed with certainty beyond the range of thirty-five yards. The boundary for small birds need not be more than sixty yards.

The size of shot for starling should be No. 8 ; for sparrows No. 10.

Before shooting a match at sparrows, the young sportsman will do well to test his gun at a mark, as to the closeness of throwing the shot.

DOG-BREAKING.

No good sport is to be had, or at least thoroughly enjoyed, with out a good dog.

The best sport with the gun, and the highest enjoyment of it, is with the best dogs.

Bad sport may often be made good with the assistance of well-bred and well-broken dogs.

It is as easy for a sportsman to select a good dog as it is for a fox-hunter to select a good horse; and the good qualities are as essential and valuable in the one as in the other.

Remember that a well-bred, well-broke, and clever dog costs no more, either for keep or tax, than an ill-bred or ill-broken mongrel.

Dog-breaking, to be entirely successful, must be conducted on rational principles. Much experience in the art is not necessary; but an acquaintance with the true nature and disposition of dogs in general will be of great service.

Neither is it by any means necessary that the breaker should be a good shot. But it is indispensable that he should be good-natured, patient, and entirely free from irascibility.

The dog-breaker who uses most kindness, and is most sparing and mild in the nature of his chastisement towards the dog, always succeeds best. The violent, severe, and impatient bully never succeeds in turning out a perfectly trained dog. The utmost he attains is to make the dog stand in terror of him; so that for fear of having some of its bones broken, or being beaten to death, it runs away on the least intimation of having done wrong; and probably puts up covey after covey as it races across the field. It is a true test, on a dog running away in this manner, that it has been badly trained and cruelly beaten. No dog which has been properly trained and mildly and judiciously chastised would do so.

It is wanton cruelty and ignorant folly to chastise a dog at any time, unless it knows why it is punished. It is a well-timed chastisement, not the severity of it, which ensures obedience.

Faults may be reproved without being punished.

Excessive flogging makes the dog hunt in fear, and with a broken spirit; whereas the bold and dauntless-spirited dog is the sportsman's pride and delight; and the courageous dog is of all others the one to hunt with most success and least fatigue. Unless a dog hunts cheerfully and willingly, entering with all its heart into the spirit of the sport, its services are not of much use.

It is true that some dogs require rather more chastisement than others; whilst some may be broken without a lash.

All dogs should be trained as much as possible by dumb signals; and this system of training is specially applicable to the instruction of pointers and setters.

A talkative trainer spoils the dog, though it be ever so well bred; because it becomes so accustomed to the voice of its trainer that it will obey none other than verbal signals. The more care and trouble the trainer takes in teaching the dog by silent signals, the more valuable and useful will it be when in pursuit of sport.

It is unreasonable to suppose that birds will lie if they hear your voice. Therefore, once more I repeat, "Don't talk to your dogs when in expectation of finding game."

A dog, in its very nature, will soon discover from its dumb trainer that, to approach game, silence must be observed. Retrievers which have been accustomed to attend sportsmen who go wild-fowl-shooting, are

11*

particularly sagacious as to their duty, and that of their master, being to observe the strictest silence: and when stalking wild-fowl, a clever dog will crawl along with belly touching the ground, on a signal to do so by its master, who probably has to do likewise.

POINTERS AND SETTERS.

There is no better age at which to commence the training of a dog than at seven months old; and all the initiatory lessons had best be given in a yard, on the premises where the dog has been brought up. The trainer will find it of immense advantage to devote about twenty minutes daily, for three or four weeks, to the preliminary lessons, before taking the dog out in the fields in search of game.

These should be given when the trainer is alone with the dog: there must be nothing to divert its attention from the trainer.

Begin by practising the dog, when hungry, to seek about the yard for pieces of food, which you have unobservedly placed in concealment: accompany the dog in its searches, encouraging it to hunt for the food by the motion of your hand; and induce the dog to fancy you are looking for something. Always show pleasure and satisfaction when the dog finds the food. Do not allow it to eat the food immediately; take it in your hand, look at it, show it to the dog, let him smell it two or three times, and then give it him to eat. Place a piece sometimes on a chair or stool, so as to induce the dog to hold up his head. The higher pointers and setters carry their noses the better, because they find their game quicker; and the birds lie better to such dogs than to those which carry their noses close to the ground. Never deceive the dog by encouraging it to hunt for a bit of food, unless there really is a piece secreted; and never allow the dog to give up until it has found it. This will go far in giving the animal early confidence in you, as possessing a superior knowledge as to whether there is game to be found or not, when in the fields.

Having taught the puppy to seek for and find the hidden pieces of food, the use of the check cord must then be resorted to, for the purpose of teaching it to stand firm, and stop instantly to the signal " to-ho !" This important lesson is taught in the following manner :—having buckled a soft leathern collar round the puppy's neck, attach thereto a cord about fifteen or twenty yards in length, the end of which you hold firmly in your hand : then encourage the dog, as be-

fore, to hunt for a piece of food; and just as its nose
is being tickled with the savor of the tidbit, call out
" to-ho !" at the same instant pulling the cord sharply,
so as to bring the dog to a stand-still; at which you
must keep him whilst you walk slowly up to him;
after which allow him to advance and eat the bit he
has found. In a short time it will be unnecessary to
use the cord, and by simply saying " to-ho !" the dog
may be instantly brought to a stand-still.

Never *throw* pieces of food to sporting puppies of
any kind; always *give it* them with the hand, and
make them take it gently.

Teaching a dog to drop to the hand, is another of
the first and most important lessons in the instruction
of pointers and setters. By " dropping to the hand"
is meant to "down charge !" or crouch to the signal
of holding up the hand high above the head. This
may be taught thoroughly in the yard, before ever
taking the dog out in the fields. The most simple
manner of teaching it is by holding up a whip, and
calling out " down charge !" Then insist on the dog
lying still whilst you walk away to another part of
the yard: if he attempts to move, tie him to a stake,
repeating your orders to " down charge." After a
very few lessons, the stake and whip may be dis-

pensed with; and the dog, by further practice, will crouch to the signal of holding up the hand, and remain so until encouraged to "hold up!" The use of the gun, first with gun-caps only, and afterwards with a very small charge of powder, will be of advantage in this lesson; taking the greatest care not to frighten the dog with a loud report, or by using the gun offensively.

Teach the dog also to obey your whistle: a single note meaning "attention;" and a continued whistle that he is to come to you. The single note should be given when the dog's attention is occupied in hunting for the secreted bits of food; and on the instant of the dog looking towards you in obedience to the whistle, direct him further by some dumb signal, either to hunt to the right or left, or to "down charge."

Never use sentences in speaking to a dog; one word only is best; more than two should never be used.

Use neither spikes nor spiked collars in dog-breaking; they are brutal instruments; which, as Colonel Hutchinson very justly remarks, "none but the most ignorant or unthinking would employ."

Having carefully inculcated the initiatory lessons alluded to, the trainer may then take the dog out in the fields; being, as before, quite alone with it. He will now require a longer check-cord than that used in the yard : if forty yards in length so much the better; and the lightest, most useful, and durable cord for the purpose is that which sailors call " ratline."

The check-cord cannot be dispensed with in dog-breaking; it is the best and only assistant the trainer requires.

The dog should now be taken to a spot where you know there is a covey of partridges; and there encouraged to hunt. If a well-bred dog, it will find and point them; and if so, walk up to the dog and pat him, saying " to-ho !" then encourage him to advance steadily; and on the birds rising, instantly check him with the cord, if he attempts to run in, by pulling him back on his haunches; but do not use the whip for the first or second attempt; nor until you find he cannot be broken of attempting to run in without using it. After you have succeeded in this important lesson, pat and reward him with a bit of food every time he does it perfectly.

Remember, also, that it is a golden rule in the instruction of a dog, to drag him back to the spot where he ought to have remained; whether for the purpose of pointing the game, or in obedience to the signal to " down charge."

Having carried the course of training thus far, you may now allow an assistant to accompany you; giving him the check-cord, whilst you use the gun and kill a few partridges: and in all probability the dog will ever after take the greatest delight in hunting for game. Be strict and prompt in checking any over-eagerness or unsteadiness; and take plenty of time in reloading after having killed a bird; and then allow the dog to find it and mouth it tenderly.

The only troublesome thing to teach in a pointer or setter is, quartering the ground: this requires perseverance and much practice. It should, strictly speaking, be done before the dog is ever taken into turnips.

The trainer must teach the dog to cross and recross the fields to the simple signal of waving the hand to right or left; and to do this effectually, at first he will have to walk with the dog, up wind, crossing and recrossing just as is required; but in time he will find it less and less necessary to do these walkings; whenever the dog skips over any portion of the ground without hunting, endeavor to make him, by signals, go and hunt it; and if he refuses or does not understand you, go yourself, good-naturedly, calling and encouraging the dog to rehunt the field.

A well distributed and judicious range, is a great accomplishment in a good dog, but difficult to teach.

Use the word "ware!" when the dog is hunting wrong, or attempting to precede you in getting over a fence or gate on entering another field.

On no account must the dog be allowed to move whilst you are reloading. Though a bird falls on open, barren ground, in the very sight of the dog, and whether killed or wounded, do not allow the pointer to go or stir after it, until you have reloaded, and given the word of encouragement. If he attempts, call him back and drag him to the place where he ought to have remained; then go yourself to the spot at which you stood when you shot the bird, and make him wait at his place whilst you reload. It is better to lose a wounded bird now and then than to allow your dog to acquire the very bad habit of running in; which he assuredly will do unless you firmly resist every attempt that he makes.

A dog having once acquired the habit of running in, it is difficult to break him of it; though in general it arises through his having been shot over by a bad shot or inexperienced sportsman, who, the moment he shoots a bird, rushes forward himself, before reloading, to secure it: I need scarcely say that such a proceeding has been the ruin of many a splendid young dog.

Many young sportsmen, on wounding a hare, are apt, in their eagerness to capture it, to encourage a pointer or retriever to chase it. Such an encouragement is also ruinous to the dog: because, after once being incited to chase, the dog will do so every time you miss. Such is the nature and instinct of the dog for chasing, that the steadiest and most perfectly trained dog may be ruined by one indiscretion of the kind.

Pointers, setters, and retrievers should never be allowed either to chase, run in, or lacerate the game. A retriever may be allowed to " road" a wounded running bird ; but the trainer must be very cautious never to allow the dogs to chase either hare or rabbit.

All dogs have a natural propensity to run after hares and rabbits ; which must be instantly restrained in such dogs as are trained to the gun.

Never use or break a young pointer, setter, or retriever, to rabbit-shooting ; it is certain ruin, and will assuredly make him a hedge-potterer all his life.

When the dog is tired, do not hunt him, it decreases his zeal for sport, and injures his constitution to encourage sport to weary limbs.

Let every sportsman who uses setters remember,

that they require water almost every hour, especially during hot weather, or they cannot endure the fatigue of a hard day's work.

A well-broken dog seldom requires a word to be addressed to it; a dumb signal, a wave of the hand or motion of the head is sufficient.

If you want to catch the dog's attention in the field, simply whistle gently, one note only; and on the dog raising his head, make your signal.

Never interrupt a dog when it appears to be on the scent of birds.

Remember too, that, although the dog be ever so well broken, if the young sportsman does not know how to hunt it and insist on its keeping to the rules of instruction inculcated by the trainer, it will soon be taking liberties; and if these are uncorrected, the dog is soon spoilt.

A thorough-bred dog which has been accustomed to work for a good shot, never works willingly for a bad shot; after discovering that he seldom kills any thing. Such a dog has often been known to run away off the field, and endeavor to find its old master.

A sportsman should never allow his dogs to jump or fawn upon him: such a liberty has been the cause of many an accident with the gun.

The term " hold up !" means, not to drop the nose too near the ground. It is also the general term used when directing the dog to range or hunt the field. They are almost the only words of encouragement that should be spoken to the pointer or setter in the field. " To-ho !" need not be used very often, and indeed never to a steady dog ; it indicates that the dog must pause until the sportsman approaches : and then, on further encouragement, advance to the precise spot where the game is lying. Some dogs grow impatient after standing a reasonable time, and then rush in upon the game ; others will stand ten minutes or more. Colonel Hutchinson relates an anecdote of a dog which was left standing in the field whilst the sportsman went to a friend's house and lunched. As it is a very good story I give it in his own words.

" The largest price that I ever knew paid for a dog was for a red setter. After mid-day he came upon a covey basking in the sun. His owner very knowingly told the shooting party that they might go to luncheon—that he would leave the dog, and accompany them, engaging that they should find him still steadily pointing on their return. The promise was faithfully redeemed by the stanch setter. One of the sportsmen was so struck with the performance, that he could not resist buying at a tremendous figure, and he soon regained, I believe, much of the purchase-money from some incredulous acquaintance, by backing the animal to perform a similar feat." This, however, is no great test of excellence; a dog that will stand very firm for many minutes may nevertheless have many failings.

When the dog is at a distance, and you wish him instantly to " down charge," thrust the hand up as high in the air as you can reach, stooping the head at the same time.

Ignorant sportsmen always roar out to the dog immediately after firing, to " down charge!" whereas a well-broken dog needs not a word to induce it to do so, the report of the gun is the only signal necessary; and when otherwise, the hand should be raised in a manner to indicate the order, which should be instantly obeyed. If the sportsman finds that his dog will not " down charge" except by having the verbal order addressed to it, he would be wise to be rid of such a dog, it shows bad and imperfect training.

False points, and pointing larks, are very bad faults; I never knew an instance in which a dog was cured of them, after thoroughly acquiring the habit.

It is highly desirable that the sportsman should break his own dog, and there can be no excuse for any country gentleman : if he has an ill-trained mongrel it is his own fault, he has plenty of time to break a young dog ; and with care and constant practice, he may make one as perfect as can be desired.

A well educated man can always train a dog very much better than an ignorant one.

In your humanity and good-nature be not too mild and sparing of the whip ; it is sometimes absolutely necessary to use it ; but the chastisement must be given with discretion.

Use few words in dog-breaking ; and fewer still when in expectation of finding game. The fewer words of command you have in dog-breaking the sooner and better they will be understood by the animal under training.

In training two dogs to hunt together, let all the single lessons be first perfected before allowing them to hunt double. When those are well learned, throw the dogs off, one to the right, and the other to the left ; and make them cross each other as they quarter the field. Never allow one to follow the other, or adopt their own ways ; but make them go by different routes, working up wind, and crossing right and left.

The sportsman should be cautious as to whom he entrusts the breaking of his dog; for although it is an easy art, it requires time and attention, with perseverance and constant practice: and, as bad habits are learned as quickly as good ones, the training and education of the dog to the gun and the field, must be carefully inculcated; for it must be remembered that bad habits in a dog are even more difficult to break than in a man.

On returning home from sport, look to the dogs' feet for thorns, and if any, extract them forthwith. Give them plenty of clean straw on a boarded floor, raised a foot or so above the ground. Never allow a dog to sleep on a bricked floor, nor in any damp place. Give them a portion of animal food with vegetables daily, when hard worked.

And bear in mind, that a dog is not able to stand two successive days' hard work so well as an active sportsman.

The dog is an excellent physiognomist, and when near enough, understands from the countenance of its master whether he is pleased or displeased with its actions.

It is sometimes evident from a dog's look and manner, that he has just been doing wrong, though his master may not, at the moment, be aware of the nature of the wrong. In such a case the master should look sternly at the dog, so as to show his displeasure; and immediately endeavor to find out the error, which if discovered at once, the dog should be punished; but, having come and confessed the fault, natural goodness and humanity demand that the chastisement should be slight.

A dog is all sincerity of heart towards its master, and knows not how to conceal a fault or mislead him. Thus the dog may have flushed a covey through carelessness, or have chased a hare, or committed some such error; in which case, whether the fault be confessed or not, unless immediately corrected, the dog will think he may do so at any time with impunity.

Sir Walter Scott says: "The Almighty who gave the dog to be the companion of our pleasures and our toils, hath invested him with a nature noble and incapable of deceit. He forgets neither friend or foe; remembers, and with accuracy, both benefit and injury. He hath a share of man's intelligence, but no share of man's falsehood. You may bribe a soldier to slay a man with his sword, or a witness to take life by false accusation; but you cannot make a hound tear his benefactor."

It sometimes happens, through the ignorance or stupidity of the sportsman, that the dog is unable to comprehend what the instructions imply, or require of him; and in sagacious modesty, he puts his tail down and comes trembling to his master's heels; telling him, through the expression of his canine countenance, that he is desirous of obliging, if the sportsman will only convey to him in the most natural and comprehensible dog-language, what his wishes are. A man who beats his dog, so failing, is a brute, and unworthy the services of so noble and intelligent a creature.

SPANIELS.

Many of the foregoing remarks, under the head "Dog-breaking," apply equally to breaking spaniels; more particularly those with reference to mild chastisement, hunting for secreted food, &c.

Spaniels are lively and indefatigable little creatures, and among the most useful dogs a sportsman can employ for certain purposes.

There is great difficulty in restraining them within bounds, or rather within range of gun-shot, unless they are carefully trained when young.

The check-cord is the most effective instrument that can be employed, and, indeed, the only one with which to break spaniels.

Whilst training young dogs, always reward their good actions with little bits of biscuit or cheese; and train dogs before feeding them, not just after. The finer the olfactory organs in a spaniel, the better dog it will make when trained.

The term " hie on!" or " hie in!" may be used to spaniels when encouraging them to hunt a thicket or hedge; but such terms should never be used either to pointers or setters.

The trainer should insist on young dogs hunting the field closely; to encourage them to do so, he should walk steadily, taking the field in zig-zag form, after the manner required by the dog; and in giving spaniels their first lessons at the fences, do not allow them to hurry over the ground, but insist on their working very close.

Never allow them to have their own way in their early lessons.

They must also be taught to drop to the hand; and

12

if intended to be used in the field for finding partridges, they must be taught to " down charge !"

RETRIEVERS.

Retrievers are most useful and valuable dogs to the
sportsman. In almost every department connected
with the sport of shooting, the services of a retriever
are essential. Much time is saved in recovering
wounded game, and many birds are brought to bag,
which, without the assistance of a retriever, would
be lost.

But there is no dog in which a greater degree of
care is required in its instruction ; for unless most
judiciously trained, the best bred animal will be a
nuisance rather than an assistance.

Mr. Folkard remarks in the " Wild Fowler," on
training a retriever, " Every thing depends on the first
lessons they receive, as to their ever being of good
service to the sportsman." A remark in which every
man who knows any thing about training a retriever
will concur ; for if once a young dog acquires a habit
of killing, biting, or lacerating wounded birds, it is
almost impossible to break him of it effectually.
Sooner or later he will again begin his bad habits. It

is, therefore, of the highest consideration that the retriever should receive its first lessons from none but those who are thoroughly awake to these important principles. A retriever which injures the birds, is an animal that no sportsman would allow to accompany him; for, of all faults, it is the very worst, and one which renders the dog useless for field sports.

The first lessons given a retriever puppy should be, to search about the yard, at home, for pieces of food which you have hidden; encouraging the dog to seek and find them, and then rewarding him with the pleasure of eating them. These lessons should be given, at first, when the dog is hungry; and always when no one is present to interrupt the trainer or the puppy.

After a little practice, as above, the trainer should, by means of a long string, drag a piece of savory food through the grass; commencing at short distances, and in a few weeks extending it to fifty or one hundred yards, encouraging the dog to follow and find it; and always rewarding him with a bit of food when he succeeds. The more the retriever puppy is practised in this way the better.

Many a retriever puppy is spoilt by children, who, innocently enough, delight in throwing sticks and stones for the dog to fetch; first spitting on them, in order (as they say), that "the dog may find it by the smell, and not bring a wrong one." The little innocents, however, unless they happen to have uncommon fetid breath, should know that the spittle is of no great assistance to the dog in retrieving their missiles.

It is astonishing how soon a young dog may be spoilt in this manner, by being taught to bring hard substances, of which it always endeavors to keep possession, though the juveniles tug away at them, and force them out of the dog's mouth with all their might. After such performances, who can wonder if the dog so tampered with, bites and lacerates the game it retrieves?

The retriever puppy should be taught to retrieve with soft substances, having nothing disagreeable about them, either in smell or appearance. A bit of stuffed fur is as good as any thing, then a stuffed bird skin, but never any thing hard or heavy.

Never praise a dog whilst bringing, wait until he has brought and deposited in your hand, then praise and pat him.

After this and the previous lessons, the dog should be taken out into the field, being led by an attendant;

whilst an elder and well-trained dog retrieves game or birds which the sportsman shoots.

As soon as possible in the field, the dog should have a winged bird to retrieve, which, if it kills or bites, it should be made to understand distinctly that it has done wrong. With angry countenance the sportsman should exhibit the torn flesh, and, unmistakably evince his displeasure by gentle chastisement with a small dog-whip.

This practice, with a live bird, should be tried over and over again, and the dog will soon acquire the habit of bringing the birds in its mouth without injuring them in the least. But should it be found difficult to prevent the dog killing or lacerating the birds, resort must be had to another expedient, viz., a pincushion studded with pins, having their points outwards. Put the pincushion in a child's sock, a cloth glove or something soft, and then frequently practise the dog in retrieving it. If the puppy is disposed to be hard-mouthed, it should have lessons in retrieving the pincushion before being taken into the field. The color of the sock or glove containing the pincushion should be frequently changed, in order that the dog may suspect every thing it touches, rather than fear to bite one particular colored object only.

It appears from that most excellent work "The Wild-fowler," that the author had a retriever puppy so carefully trained in this respect, that on its first lesson in the fens, in retrieving a wild duck which was only slightly wounded, so tenderly did the puppy gripe it, that the bird freed itself from the jaws of its young captor; leaving, as it flew away, only a few feathers in the dog's mouth.   There is a beautiful engraving of this most striking scene in the work alluded to; and it is stated that the dog never afterwards allowed a captive to escape.   It was, truly, a most promising error in a puppy, and one which needed no chastisement; the dog was vexed enough, no doubt, to lose so pleasing a prize, as probably the sportsman would be also, though he must have rejoiced at the perfectly successful training of his puppy retriever.

There is no doubt but retrievers thoroughly delight in bringing birds in their mouths; and when trained to bring them alive without hurting them, their delight is increased as they become more practised.

If the retriever is required for snipe or wild-fowl shooting, it should be taught in summer to retrieve from the water; and afterwards, when well learned,

be the weather ever so cold, the dog will not refuse to enter the water in pursuit of a dead or
wounded bird.

Retrievers should be taught to deliver the game
into the sportsman's hand, or directly at his feet;
and they must be restrained from running in, by
practising them in the "down charge" lesson, in
the same manner as with pointers and setters (see
ante, p. 252.)

The retriever should always be taught to keep
close to his master when in the field, until directed
to "fetch." It will then learn, in course of time, to
watch the birds as they fall to the gun; and on a
signal from its master, go direct to the spot.

When a dead or wounded bird is lost, the dog
should be encouraged to search diligently for it, the
terms "seek!" or "hie lost!" being sometimes used;
though most dogs that are well trained and have
good noses, hunt best without any such encouragement.

About two months of careful instruction is sufficient to break a retriever, and render it useful for
land or water; but it can only be perfected by time
and practice.

Close confinement, without air and exercise, is

prejudicial to the dog's health: and ultimately impairs its sagacity and spoils its temper.

During the non-shooting season dogs should be taken out almost every day with a trustworthy person.

They require watching, lest children or servants tamper with them, by sending them to and fro to retrieve stones and sticks.

Never use a retriever for killing vermin.

It is not a good plan to kennel retrievers with other dogs.

And if allowed to run at large, they are in danger of being spoilt by idle persons.

The sportsman should never use two retrievers at once; one is at all times sufficient. By using two in the same sport, both are so eager for the honor of retrieving the bird, that one struggles to take it away from the other, and so the bird is sure to be torn and spoilt. When it accidentally occurs that two dogs are so situated, the sportsman should spare the dog which first captured the bird, and chastise the other; more particularly if the other be not a retriever.

Train the retriever (as indeed all dogs for shooting) as much as possible by silent signals; use the voice seldom; and when necessary to speak to the dog, do so with one word only, or two at the most.

APPENDIX.

GAME LAWS OF THE STATE OF NEW YORK.

AN ACT TO AMEND AN ACT ENTITLED "AN ACT TO AMEND AND CONSOLIDATE THE SEVERAL ACTS RELATING TO THE PRESERVA-TION OF MOOSE, WILD DEER, BIRDS, AND FRESH-WATER FISH," PASSED MAY NINTH, EIGHTEEN HUNDRED AND SIXTY-EIGHT.

Passed May 18, 1869.

The People of the State of New York, represented in Senate and Assembly, do enact as follows:—

SECTION 1. No person shall kill, or pursue with intent to kill, in the counties of Kings, Queens, or Suffolk, any moose or wild deer at any time within five years after the passage of this act, and in the residue of the State only during the months of August, from the fifteenth day thereof, September, October, November, and December, or shall expose for sale, or have in his or her possession, any green moose or deer skin, or fresh venison, save only in the months aforesaid and to the tenth of January. The hunting of deer with dogs is hereby prohibited.

12*

§ 2. No person shall at any time kill any wild fawn during the periods when such fawn is in its spotted coat, or kill, expose for sale, or have at any time in his or her possession any gray rabbit, from the first of January to the first of Novembe

§ 3. No person shall kill, catch, or discharge any fire-arm at any wild pigeon while in any nesting-ground, or break up or in any manner disturb such nesting-ground or the nests, or birds therein, or discharge any fire-arm at any distance within one-fourth mile of such nesting-place at such pigeon.

§ 4. No person shall kill or expose for sale, or have in his possession after the same is killed, any wood duck (sometimes called summer duck), dusky duck (commonly called black duck), mallard or teal duck, between the first day of February and the fifteenth day of August, in each year, except on the waters of Long Island Sound or the Atlantic Ocean. No person shall at any time kill any wild duck, goose, or other wild fowl, with or by means of the device or instrument known as the swivel or punt gun, or with or by means of any gun other than such guns as are habitually raised at arm's length, and fired from the shoulder, or shall use any such device or instrument or gun other than such gun as aforesaid, with intent to kill any such duck, goose, or other wild fowl. No person shall in any manner kill, or molest with intent to kill, any wild ducks, geese, or other wild fowl, while the same are sitting at night upon their resting-places.

§ 5. Any person violating the foregoing provisions of this act shall be deemed guilty of a misdemeanor, and shall likewise be liable to a penalty of fifty dollars for each offence; and it shall be the duty of all sheriffs, constables,.and other police officers to see that these provisions are enforced.

§ 6. No person shall at any time, within this State, kill or trap, or expose for sale, or have in his possession after the same is killed, any eagle, fish hawk, night hawk, whippoorwill, finch, sparrow, yellow bird, wren, martin, swallow, tanager, oriole, bobolink, or any other song-bird; or kill, trap, or expose for sale, any robin, brown thresher, woodpecker, black-bird, meadow lark, or starling, save during the months of August, September, October, November, and December; nor destroy or rob the nests of any wild birds whatever, under a penalty of five dollars for each bird so killed, trapped, or exposed for sale, and for each nest destroyed or robbed. This section shall not apply to any person who shall kill or trap any bird for the purpose of studying its habits or history, or having the same stuffed and set up as a specimen; nor to any person who shall kill on his own premises any robins during the period when summer fruits or grapes are ripening, provided such robin is killed in the act of destroying such fruits or grapes.

§ 7. No person snall, at any time within ten years from the passage of this act, kill any pinnated grouse, commonly called the prairie fowl, unless upon grounds owned by them, and grouse placed thereon by said owners, under a penalty of ten dollars for each bird so killed.

§ 8. No person shall kill, or have in his or her possession, except alive, for the purpose of preserving the same alive through the winter, or expose for sale, any woodcock, between the first day of January and the fourth day of July, or any quail, sometimes called Virginia partridge, between the first day of January and the twentieth day of October, or any ruffed grouse, commonly called partridge, between the first day of January and the first day of September, or have in his possession any pinnated grouse, commonly called prairie chicken, or expose the same for sale between the first day of February and the first day of July, under a penalty of ten dollars for each bird so killed or had in possession, or exposed for sale.

§ 9. No person shall kill, or pursue with intent to kill, in the counties of Kings, Queens, Suffolk, and Richmond, any ruffed grouse, commonly called partridge, or any Virginia partridge, commonly called quail, at any time within two years after the passage of this act, except such person has stocked with game-birds any of the lands lying therein, and they only under such restrictions as are contained in the various sections of this act.

§ 10. No person shall, at any time or in any place within this State, with any trap or snare, take any quail or ruffed grouse, under a penalty of five dollars for each quail or grouse so trapped or snared.

§ 11. There shall be no shooting, hunting, or trapping on the first day of the week, called Sunday; and any person violating the provisions of this section shall be liable to a penalty of not more than twenty-five nor less than ten dollars for each offence, or imprisonment for not more than twenty nor less than five days.

§ 12. In the counties of Kings, Queens, and Suffolk, or on the waters adjacent to the same, no person shall kill, or have in his or her possession after the same is killed, any wild goose, brant, wood duck, dusky duck (commonly called black duck), mallard, widgeon, teal, shelldrake, broadbill, coot, or old squaw, between the tenth day of June and the twentieth day of October in each year ; and no person shall kill or shoot at any wild goose, brant, or duck after sunset and before daylight on any day of the year ; and no person shall sail for wild fowl or shoot at any wild goose, brant, or duck from any vessel propelled by sail or steam, or from any boat attached to the same ; and no person shall use any floating battery or machine for the purpose of killing wild fowl, or shoot out of such floating machine at any wild goose, brant, or duck. But nothing herein contained shall prohibit the use of floats or batteries in Long Island Sound. Any person violating any of the provisions of this section shall be liable to a penalty of fifty dollars for each offence.

§ 13. Any person trespassing upon lands owned or occupied by another, for the purpose of shooting, hunting, or fishing thereon, after public notice by such owner or occupant, as provided in the following section, shall be deemed guilty of trespass, and shall be liable to such owner or occupant in exemplary damages for each offence, not exceeding twenty-five dollars, and shall also be liable to the owner or occupant for the value of the game killed or taken.

§ 14. The notice referred to in the preceding section shall be given by publishing an advertisement particularly describing such land, and forbidding such trespass, in the official papers of the county, or a paper published in the town where such lands are situated, for the period of three weeks, and in the months of April or May in each year, by sign-boards at least one foot square, to be put up and maintained in not less than two conspicuous places on the premises; such notices to be signed by or have appended thereto the name of the owner or occupant.

§ 15. No person shall place in any fresh-water stream, lake, or pond, without the consent of the owner, or in shore waters and estuaries with rivers debouching into them, any lime or other deleterious substance, with the intent to injure fish; or any drug or medicated bait, with intent thereby to poison or catch fish; nor place in any pond or lake stocked with or inhabited by trout or black bass, any drug or other deleterious substance, with intent to destroy such trout or bass; nor place in any fresh-water pond or stream stocked with brook trout, any pike, pickerel, black bass, or rock bass, or other piscivorous fish (salmon excepted), without the consent of the owner or owners of the lands upon which such pond or stream is situated. Any person violating the provisions of this section shall be deemed guilty of a misdemeanor, and shall, in addition thereto, and in addition to any damage he may have done, be liable to a penalty of one hundred dollars.

§ 16. Every person building or maintaining a dam upon any of the fluvial waters of this State, which dam is higher than two feet, shall likewise build and maintain, during the months of March, April, May, September, October, and November, for the purpose of the passage of fish, a sluiceway in the mid-channel, at least one foot in depth at the edge of the dam, and of proper width, and placed at an angle of not more than thirty degrees, and extending entirely to the running water below the dam, which sluiceway shall be protected on each side by an apron at least one foot in height to confine the water therein.

§ 17. No person shall at any time, with intent so to do, catch any speckled brook trout or any speckled river trout, with any device save only with a hook and line; and no person shall catch any such trout, or have any such trout in his or her possession, save only during the months of April, May, June, July, and August, under a penalty of five dollars for each trout so caught or had in his possession; but this section shall not prevent any person or corporation from catching trout in waters owned by them or upon their premises to stock other waters, in any manner or at any time. But the counties of Kings, Queens, and Suffolk shall be excepted from the provisions of the above section, so far as to allow the taking or catching of trout in the counties last named during the month of March.

§ 18. Any person or persons or company, engaged in the increase of brook trout by artificial process (known as fish culture), may take from their own ponds, in any way, and cause to be transported, and may sell brook trout and the spawn of brook trout at any time, and common carriers may transport them, and dealers sell them, on condition that the packages thereof so transported are accompanied by a certificate of a justice of the peace, certifying that such trout are sent by the owner or owners or agent of parties so engaged in fish culture. And such persons or company may take, in any way, and at any time, upon the premises of any person, under permission of the owner thereof, brook trout to be kept and used as brook trout for artificial propagation only, and for no other purpose.

§ 19. No person shall take or have in possession any salmon or lake trout in the months of November, December, January, and February, under a penalty of five dollars for each fish so taken and had in possession. But this section shall not apply to the waters of Otsego Lake.

§ 20. No person shall take or have in possession any Oswego bass or black bass, or muscallonge, between the first day of January and the first day of

May, under a penalty of five dollars for each fish so taken or had in possession. And no person shall take any black bass from the waters of Lake Mahopac, or have in possession any fish so taken, between the first day of January and the first day of July, under a penalty of ten dollars for each fish so taken or had in possession.

§ 21. No person shall, at any time, take any fish with a net, spear, or trap of any kind, or set any trap, net, weir, or pot, with intent to catch fish, in any of the fresh waters or canals of this State, except as hereinbefore or hereinafter provided; nor shall it be lawful, at any time, to draw any seine or net, for the taking of fish, in any portion of Flushing Bay or its branches, nor in lakes Canandaigua, Cayuga, Onondaga, Champlain, or the inlets thereof; and any person violating the provisions of this section shall be deemed guilty of a misdemeanor, and shall likewise be liable to a penalty of twenty-five dollars for each offence; but suckers, catfish, bullheads, bony fish, or moss bunkers, eels, white fish, shad, herring, and minnows are exempted from the operation of this section, also pike in all waters save those lying in Columbia County; provided, however, that nothing in this section shall be so construed as to legalize the use of gill nets in any of the inland waters or canals of this State, nor seines or nets of any kind in the waters of Otsego Lake, except from the first day of March to the last day of August, and no gill nets except during the months of July and August. But no

such seine or net shall have meshes less than one inch
and one-quarter in size, and in the Hudson River the
meshes of all gill nets shall be five inches in size
each, and those of fykes set in any of the waters surrounding Long Island, Fire Island, Staten Island, and
the bays, salt-water estuaries and rivers approaching thereto, to be not less than five inches each in
size; and any person who shall wilfully injure or destroy, by grappling or otherwise, any nets used in
the Hudson or East rivers for the purpose of catching shad, shall be liable to a penalty of twenty-five
dollars for each offence, and in default of payment
· thereof, shall be imprisoned in the county jail of the
county within whose jurisdiction the offence may be
committed.

§ 22. No person shall sell, expose for sale, or purchase, or have in his or her possession, any fish taken
contrary to the preceding section of this act, under a
penalty of five dollars for each fish so sold, exposed
for sale, purchased, or had in possession with intent
to violate the provisions of this act.

§ 23. It shall not be lawful for any person to take
and retain with a seine or net in any of the waters
of Jamaica Bay, or in any of the creeks or channels
connecting the said bay with the ocean, nor in
Haunces Creek, in Hempstead Bay, any fish known
as sheep's head, under a penalty of twenty dollars,
or imprisonment not less than ten days for each
sheep's head so taken with a seine or net. Suits for
the recovery of the penalties incurred for a violation

of this section may be brought before any justice of
the peace whose jurisdiction extends to the shores of
said Jamaica Bay.

§ 24. All penalties imposed under the provisions
of this act may be recovered with cost of suit by any
person or persons in his or their own names, before
any justice of the peace in the county where the
offence was committed or where the defendant re-
sides; or when such suit shall be brought in the city
of New York, before any justice of any of the district courts or of the Marine Court of said city; or
such penalties may be recovered in an action in the
Supreme Court of this State by any person or persons,
in his or their own names, which action shall be gov-
erned by the same rules as other actions in said Supreme Court, except that on a recovery by the plaintiff or plaintiffs in such suit in said court of less than
fifty dollars the plaintiff shall be entitled to costs not
exceeding the amount of such recovery; and any
district court judge, justice of the peace, police or
other magistrate, is authorized, upon receiving sufficient security for costs on the part of the complain-
ant, and sufficient proof, by affidavit, of the violation
of the provisions of this act by any person being
temporarily within his jurisdiction, but not residing
therein, or by any person whose name and residence
are unknown, to issue his warrant, and have such
offender committed or held to bail to answer the
charge against him; and any district court judge,
justice of the peace, police or other magistrate may,

upon proof of probable cause to believe in the concealment of any game or. fish mentioned in this act, during any of the prohibited periods, issue his search-warrant and cause search to be made in any house, market, boat, car, or other building, and for that end may cause any apartment, chest, box, locker, or crate to be broken open and the contents examined. Any penalties, when collected, shall be paid by the court before which recovery shall be had, one-half to the overseers of the poor, for the use of the poor of the town in which conviction is had, and the remainder to the prosecutor. On the non-payment of the penalty the defendants shall be committed to the common jail of the county for a period not less than five days, and at the rate of one day for each dollar of the amount of the judgment, where the sum is over five dollars in amount. Any court of special sessions in this State shall have jurisdiction to try and dispose of all and any of the offences arising in the same county against the provisions of this act; and every justice of the peace shall have jurisdiction within his county of actions to recover any penalty hereby given or created.

§ 25. Any person proving that the birds, fish, skins, or animals found in his or her possession during the prohibited periods were imported from beyond the United States, or were killed prior to such periods, or were killed in any place outside the limits of this State, but within the United States, and that the law of such place did not prohibit such killing, shall be exempted from the penalties of this act. Except that any person having in his or her possession pinnated grouse, commonly called prairie-chickens, ruffed grouse, commonly called partridges, fresh venison, or quail, on or after the first day of March, and between that day and the time when they can be lawfully killed under the provisions of this act, shall be liable to the penalties hereinbefore set forth, regardless of the time when or place where the said game was killed.

§ 26. In all prosecutions under this act, it shall be competent for common carriers or express companies to show that the inhibited article in his or her possession came into such possession in another State, or from beyond the United States, in which State the law did not prohibit such possession, and such showing shall be deemed a defence in such prosecution. No action for a penalty under the provisions of this act shall be settled or compromised, except upon the payment into court of the full amount of such penalty, unless upon such terms and conditions as may be imposed by the district attorney of the county in which such action shall have been brought.

§ 27. Nothing in this act contained shall apply to fish caught or to the taking of fish in the waters of Lake Ontario, or any of its bays or estuaries within the counties of Oswego, Jefferson, Cayuga, Wayne, and St. Lawrence, nor to the catching of fish in any way in the St. Lawrence River.

§ 28. The provisions of this act shall not be deemed to apply or affect the taking of fish in Oneida Lake, at a distance of one mile beyond the shores thereof, or prevent the taking of fish from Sand Pond or Moss Lake and Fern Lake, lying in the county of Ulster, by the owner or owners of the lands upon which said lakes are situated, during the month of September.

§ 29. It shall be unlawful to use or draw for the taking of fish of any kind whatever, any seine or net in Kennyetto or Fondasbush Creek, in the county of Fulton, or in the Sacandaga Vlaie, or in any part thereof, in said county, above the covered bridge, near the village of Fish House, commonly known as the " Vlaie Creek Bridge," or any of the streams emptying into the said Vlaie.

§ 30. Any person violating the provisions of the preceding section shall, upon conviction thereof, be deemed guilty of misdemeanor, and also liable to a penalty of twenty-five dollars, which may be recovered in the manner prescribed in section twenty of said chapter eight hundred and eighty-eight, hereby amended.

§ 31. All acts and parts of acts inconsistent with the provisions of this act are hereby repealed.

§ 32. This act shall take effect on the first day of June, eighteen hundred and sixty-nine.